NO TIME TO RUN

ROCKFORD SECURITY MYSTERY SERIES

L. A. DOBBS

1
———

Alison James slid the card she'd been dealt in front of her and waited for the dealer to finish the round. The casino had an energized vibe, the cool oxygenated air helping to keep everyone alert and eager to spend more money. Gamblers dotted the green felt tables. The pro's studied their hands with blank faces. The tourists, with their free drinks in front of them, showed more emotion. Alison could tell at a glance which ones had been dealt good hands and which had busted.

Alison let the steady clanging of the slots and the din of voices fade into the background as she kept one eye on the cards and the other on the crowd. The place wasn't filled to capacity, which suited Alison just fine. She preferred to come when it was only moderately crowded. Less people to keep track of that way. Less faces in the crowd to scrutinize. Less chance of one of *them* spotting her before she spotted them.

Shifting in her chair, she shot a sideways glance at the stranger beside her. He looked maybe sixty and almost as wide as he was tall. Didn't matter what he looked like, really, just that he was there. Having other people at the blackjack table made counting the cards easier, especially tonight.

Tonight, she needed all the distraction she could get while she calculated her odds.

She'd chosen the Lucky Ace because she'd expected it to be sedate, safe, secure. The new owners had proclaimed a war on crime in the place, which usually equated to less crowds and more opportunities to win. Not tonight, however.

Tonight the place was crawling with extra security. That made her nervous and when Alison was nervous she tended to get chatty with math jokes.

"What do you call a number that can't keep still?"

The man looked at her out of the corner of his eye, gave a half shrug and focused back on his cards.

Disappointed her fellow gambler didn't seem interested in her punch line, Alison went to give him her signature hair over the shoulder flip, but encountered only air. *Well, damn.* She'd forgotten that she'd taken to wearing her new longer hairstyle of auburn curls in a ponytail. That would still take some getting used to.

Then again, considering everything in her life was

different now, it *all* still took some getting used to. Determined to keep her fellow player distracted and not allow him to get too suspicious about her, or too curious about her recent winning streak, Alison laid the punch line on him anyway. "A roamin' numeral."

He gave her a flat look and she snorted, raising a brow at him. "Get it? A Roman numeral."

The jokes were her quirk, the one she just couldn't seem to leave behind. A piece of her past that she could safely allow out in the open since most people didn't get her mathlete-type humor anyway.

"Hit me," Mr. Hefty said, inching away from her slightly.

She gave him a side glance and crossed her legs in the opposite direction.

Gutsy move, ordering up another card. She quickly tallied the numbers in her head. The guy had sixteen showing. Based on the cards in her hand, his chances of going over twenty-one with the next draw were eighty-four-point-five to one. Alison glanced up at the dealer, a friend of hers named Faye, and winked.

Faye maintained her usual cool demeanor and slid another card from the deck, positioning it in front of Mr. Hefty before flipping it over.

Ha! Jack of Diamonds. Busted.

"Shit." The guy pushed his sizable bulk away from the table, grabbed the chips in front of him and took off, mumbling under his breath about bad jokes and bad luck.

"Guess he didn't appreciate my humor." Alison watched the guy walk away then ordered up one last card from Faye, smiling as her friend turned it over to reveal an Ace of Clubs to go with her two Kings.

Blackjack. Just like I'd planned.

Faye grinned and shook her head, her long chestnut brown hair gleaming beneath the recessed lighting. She passed Alison a stack of chips to add to her already over-flowing winnings for the night. "Guess not."

Two beefy security guards passed behind Alison, and she quickly glanced at them while stacking her chips. "Something going on?"

"Don't know." Faye straightened then stretched her lower back, the arch of her spine highlighting her generous curves and drawing the attention of several appreciative male patrons at the adjacent tables. "I heard the new owner and her boyfriend are in tonight to check up on things. Maybe that's got something to do with it." With only Alison at the table now, Faye relaxed her professional persona a bit and rested one hand on her hip while leaning the other on the table's edge. "Too bad, if you ask me. All this extra muscle, means they pulled Rockford McHottie off the floor. And I'm missing my nightly eye candy something fierce."

Alison raised a brow at the way her friend's Latino accent rolled the R in Rockford, making it sound risqué.

Good old, Faye. Always up for a party or a hot man. "Rockford McHottie, huh? Is that his official title?"

"To me it is." Faye futzed with the front of her uniform a bit before leaning over and lowering her voice. A collective hush fell over the male players nearby as the low-cut white shirt beneath Faye's standard, casino-issue vest showed a provocative glimpse of flesh. Faye seemed completely oblivious, but Alison knew better. She used her looks the same way Alison used her brains—to survive and thrive. "Everyone else calls him Owen Rockford, the head of casino security. Have you seen him?"

"No." Alison rearranged the stacks of plastic colored chips in front of her for the umpteenth time and frowned. She had better things to pay attention to in here, like someone recognizing her from her past. "Why would I care anyway?"

"Because he's gorgeous."

In her experience, gorgeous men got you nowhere but trouble. More guards followed the same path as the first two and a fresh sprout of unease blossomed in Alison's gut. "Considering all these goons running around, maybe they should've kept their head security honcho on the floor."

"I know, right?" Faye gave a small shrug. "Even if there was a problem, though, it's not like they'd tell me anyway. I'm just a dealer. Small potatoes in the bigger scheme of things. But you can bet if it were up to me, I'd make sure Owen was down here every night. Preferably with stubble and a G-string. Nothing else."

"Nice." Alison chuckled. "How would that help with safety? Where would he put his gun?"

"I know exactly where he could store his weapon, Chica." Faye gave her a saucy wink. "And safety isn't exactly my top priority when there's hot guys around, as you well know."

One of the pit managers passed by their table and gave Faye a disparaging once over before moving on. Faye straightened immediately and adjusted her uniform back into pristine condition before taking her appointed spot again. "Would you like another round, ma'am?"

"What I'd like is to know what the hell has things so tense in here."

"Like I said, I'm not sure. But you're right. Things do seem more high-strung than usual." Faye's dark gaze darted around the room before returning to Alison's. "There's been a normal drop in business, what with losing all the low-life drug dealers and loan sharks from the premises, but I've never seen quite such high security here on such a slow night. Are you sure you don't want to play one more round? You're on a winning streak, Chica."

"No, thanks." Alison stood and took her chips in hand. Her success was exactly the problem. If she got caught counting cards, it would bring unwanted attention. Unwanted attention might mean an end to her privacy, and privacy was her top priority right now. Privacy kept her alive.

"See you later." She waved to her friend and headed for the bathroom. She didn't really need to use it, but the bathrooms had no cameras and it was part of her overly-cautious plan to reduce the chance of being tracked on surveillance. It was probably over-kill, but one could never be too sure. So, she usually spent twenty minutes in the bathroom, or headed to the eating areas or any other area that didn't have cameras. Sometimes she did both to make it even more confusing for anyone to track her. *Then* she cashed out.

Forty minutes later, she approached the cashier kiosk in the middle of the large room. The Lucky Ace had been recently renovated, following the new owners taking over. You could still smell a faint hint of fresh paint and drywall in the air. Plus, they'd brightened the interior by adding more lighting and removing some of the old-school furnishings, replacing them with comfortable, modern, more contemporary styling. The place still retained its Old Vegas feel, it was now just less mob hangout and more vintage hipster refuge.

As she waited in line to cash in her chips, Alison eyed the exits and counted the guards in place. At least twenty that she could spot, and those were only the uniformed guys. Her count didn't include plain clothes officers and undercover private security. She rolled her tense neck and shuffled her feet in place. There had to be some reason for all the extra muscle. She believed Faye honestly didn't know, but not having all the answers didn't sit well with her analytical brain. She wanted to know all the angles, solve all the equations, in order to stay safe, to stay one step ahead, to stay breathing.

Yet another guard sidled past her and bumped her arm. A shiver of fear passed through her at the contact. *What if they're really here for me? Have they finally found me?* A quick run of the logistics in her head helped ease her anxiety. No. If she'd been discovered, they'd call in professional reinforcements—hired thugs, trained assassins.

"How may I help you?" the cashier said, her voice even and cheerful.

Trembling slightly, Alison stepped forward and passed two stacks of hundred dollar chips through the window. "I'd like to cash these in, please?"

"Certainly, ma'am. I'll need to see some ID or your player's club card."

Familiar stress constricted her chest as Alison forced herself to breath and smile while pulling out her wallet and extracting her Nevada driver's license.

"Perfect, Ms. Smyth. One moment while I process your transaction."

She'd been through this hundreds of times—thousands, more accurately—in the past few years, but each time someone asked to see her ID it still rankled. She kept a myriad of fake licenses and passports in the small bag near her hip for just such occasions, but still. Each time she flashed one she risked discovery of her real identity

The day that happened, she'd have to flee again.

A small commotion started near the Lucky Ace's front entrance as a broke slot player tried to hightail it out of the casino with someone else's winnings and Alison's pulse skyrocketed. She glanced back at the cashier, who still typed something into a computer near the back wall. *What's taking so long? Maybe I should just leave without the money. Do I have enough in savings to...*

"Here we are, Ms. Smyth." The cashier passed back Alison's ID. "Do you have a preference in denominations?"

"Hundreds are fine."

"Very good." The woman proceeded to count out two thousand dollars in cash. "Anything else I can do for you this evening?"

"No, thanks." Alison tucked her money and ID back in her bag then turned to leave, only to be halted by the cashier's voice.

"Thank you for playing at the Lucky Ace Casino, ma'am. Good luck!"

As she hustled toward the side exit of the casino, desperate for fresh air and freedom, Alison knew she needed all the luck she could get right about now.

OWEN ROCKFORD GAZED into the chocolate brown eyes in front of him and steeled his resolve. The dog was cute, golden brown coat, happy puppy smile and those loving, trusting liquid brown eyes. But he didn't have time for a dog. He'd learned long ago never to get attached. Not to a dog or any other living creature. Getting attached meant getting hurt.

He didn't have time for a dog, anyway. Since his discharge from the military, he'd thrown all his energy into his job as head of security at the Lucky Ace Casino. The job took all his time. Not that it was a requirement, but Owen liked it that way. It saved him from having extra time for relationships and socializing. Relationships and social activities were things that Owen never intended to participate in again.

He crossed his arms over his chest as if to ward off the dog's affections. His black custom-made suit-jacket pulled tight across his upper back. Owen preferred to wear cargo pants and tee-shirts, but the suit was a consolation to the job. Never mind that he had to spend a fortune to have them custom made in order to accommodate his broad shoulders and large biceps.

As if sensing his intentions, the dog put her head in his lap and glanced up pleadingly, tugging at Owens heart. He wouldn't be a good dog owner, he spent most of his time in the casino and the rules were no dogs allowed. And Owen was a stickler for the rules.

His gaze drifted up to his new boss Shelby Bryant who was watching the two of them intently.

"She likes you," Shelby said from behind her desk.

If Owen didn't know better, he'd think his new boss had called him here just to get him to meet Peaches, the dog panting cheerfully at his feet. Besides taking over the casino that had belonged to her late father, Shelby also ran a local animal shelter called Paws and Play.

He glanced at Chase Evans, Shelby's fiancé—a former ex-con turned law student once more, now that his record had been expunged. "Seems she does, but I don't have time for a pet right now."

"Is that so?" Shelby adjusted a framed portrait of her and her father that took up one corner of her desk. She'd wasted no time in making the place her own in the last six months. Fresh paint, more modern, contemporary décor, lots of pastel upholstery and pillows and family pictures hanging on the walls.

Shelby leaned forward and folded her hands atop the desk. "That's interesting to hear you say, because I have it on good authority your new employer allows pets in the workplace under certain conditions. One of the perks of being management." She pointed to a parrot in a cage near the far corner of the large office and a cat snoozing on a nearby settee. "And Peaches has all sorts of hidden talents. If, say, you wanted to institute a drug-sniffing program here at the casino, she'd be part of the security program too."

"Seriously?" Owen chuckled. He adored Shelby and was happy to follow her orders in an employer-employee capacity, but this went way beyond those boundaries. "That's why I'm here?" He glanced at Chase for support. "You're trying to foist one of your strays on me?"

"Hey, man." Chase moved in beside his betrothed and placed his hand on her shoulder. "I get it, trust me. Shelby can be quite persistent. Almost as bad as Blake these days, always trying to fix people up. Except with her, it's pets, not other humans."

Shelby smacked him on the arm and frowned. "I'm doing no such thing, though you shouldn't complain. Blake's the reason we met, remember?"

"How could I forget?" He rubbed his forearm where she'd slapped him. "You won't let me."

"Oh, you'll pay for that one, mister." She gave her fiancé a teasing, stern look before turning back to Owen. "Honestly, you should have a trial run with Peaches. Take her home for a night or two and see how you get along. I really do think you guys would be a good match."

"Shelby..." Owen used his best warning tone and she sighed.

"Okay. Fine. Whatever. I'll take the dog back to the shelter with me later, but don't say I didn't try." Shelby crossed her arms and leaned back in her chair. "So, bring me up to date on the casino security."

Back on familiar territory, Owen launched into a litany of improvements they'd made since Shelby's last visit. Her father, Warren Bryant, had used the Lucky Ace as a front to run several less-than-lawful pursuits, but now everything was on the up-and-up and the future for the old place looked bright.

"The crews finished installing all the new cameras, meaning now we've got coverage on every square inch of the floor and the exterior. That ought to stop what's left of the dealing in the alleys behind this place."

"Good." Chase took a seat in the chair beside Owen's. "What about the police? Are they still game to partner with us to eradicate what's left of the ring my brother was with?"

"Yep." Owen shifted slightly to face him. The guy had been through a lot because of his younger brother, Shane, and his trafficking, including five years in prison for crimes he didn't commit. Owen wasn't immune to family loyalty, but Chase had taken it to a whole new extreme. Now, at least, he seemed a lot wiser and happier since he'd gotten his life back on track. "Of course, there's been a corresponding dip in revenue, with the loss of the criminal element, but I think in the long run we'll regain the tourist traffic we lost because of it."

"Me too," Shelby said. "I want to play that up in our

new advertising campaigns too. The Lucky Ace—safest spot in Vegas for vacationers or something."

"Ugh. Might want to leave the ad copy to the professionals, baby." Chase said earning another glare from Shelby.

Owen cut in to get the discussion back on track. "Anyway, with the extra funding you budgeted, I've addressed some problem areas on my staff and hired a few new guards as well. Once we get them trained, we'll be back to full capacity, just like the old days."

"Awesome." Shelby's blue eyes twinkled. "Which means you'll have more free time, right? You put in way too many hours, Owen. Not that I haven't appreciated all your help and support during the transition, but it's not healthy. You should take a vacation once all of this is running smoothly again."

Vacation? It's been so long I've forgotten the meaning of the word. First the Marines, then this place, then...

He shook his head and crossed his legs. "Nah. I wouldn't know what to do with myself."

"Well, maybe if you had a companion. You know, someone or something to keep you busy, like a pet or—"

"I knew it! I knew you wouldn't give up so easy." He glanced over at Peaches, who woofed low and watched him with full puppy glee. "Listen, girl. I'm sorry, but I just can't take you home with me."

As if in response, the dog lay down and covered her face with her front paws.

"Now look what you've done." Shelby came around the desk to crouch beside Peaches, cooing and rubbing the top of her head. "Her feelings are hurt. You two are clearly meant for each other, Owen."

Cursing under his breath, he sat forward and scratched the dog behind her floppy ears again. "I'm sorry, girl. Really I am." Shelby gave him a perturbed look and Owen relented. "Okay, fine. You can come home with me for a few days, just to see how it might work out, but no promises, all right?"

As if in answer, Peaches rolled over on top of Owen's feet, exposing her belly for a rub.

"I'll take that as a yes." He laughed. Of course the new, first woman in his life in years wasn't shy about demanding attention. That seemed to be his type anyway, at least it had been with Janine. She'd been all over him like crust on toast. Until he'd refused to give her what she wanted. Then...

Sighing he sat back while Peaches wiggled her back atop his shoes, all lolling tongue and playful pup. This hadn't been his wisest choice. Him and females of any sort or species weren't a good idea. He should've learned his lesson by now. He was better off alone, better focusing on work and not getting involved.

Shelby rocked back on her heels and grinned from ear to ear, clapping. "Fantastic! I brought the paperwork with me, just in case." She straightened and grabbed a clipboard from her desk. "Fill these out and Peaches is all yours for the next forty-eight hours. I promise, you won't be sorry."

Owen exhaled and stared at the forms, Shelby's words echoing alongside the memories in his head.

You won't be sorry...

Unfortunately, he already was.

In ways that would take far too long to explain.

2

Owen made his way back to his office at the Lucky Ace, looking forward to a couple of hours alone to collect his thoughts and finish some paperwork. Shelby said she'd drop Peaches off on her way out later, once she'd finalized all the paperwork. His plans were shattered, however, when he found his path blocked by a six-foot-plus headache and his new green companion.

"Hey, cuz." Blake Rockford leaned one shoulder against the wall while his pet iguana, Henry, perched on the other. His body language appeared relaxed, but his expression looked irritated. "I wondered where you were."

"Sorry." Owen gave him an annoyed stare and swiped his security card through the lock on the door. Blake owned Rockford Security, the firm that oversaw the security at the Lucky Ace. Technically Blake was his boss, but that still didn't mean that he should just show up and expect Owen to drop everything to accommodate him. He knew Blake didn't have an appointment. With his crazy schedule, Owen lived and died by his calendar these days and he would've remembered. He stepped inside then gestured for his cousin to follow, the eco-friendly lighting system clicking on automatically as it sensed their body heat. "I had a meeting. Been waiting long?"

"Long enough."

Blake strode over and took a seat in front of Owen's desk like he owned the place. Owen lingered near the door and shook his head. *Family. Jeez.* He smoothed a hand down the lapel of his suit and forced a smile. "So what can I do for you?"

"I reviewed some recent Lucky Ace security footage and may have found something."

"I see." Owen took his seat behind the desk, doing his best to keep the exasperation from his tone. Sure, Blake was his boss, the head honcho of Rockford Security, but all Owen wanted right now was peace and quiet, not Blake nosing into his job. "Don't you have a whole team of people to do that for you?"

"I still like to keep an eye on things myself. Two sets of eyes are better than one." Blake cooed to the lizard, who'd now climbed down onto the new leather uphol-stered arm of the chair then cocked his head toward the small viewing room attached to Owen's office. If that thing's claws ripped his new furniture to shreds, Shelby would have his hide. Blake seemed completely oblivious. "If you have a minute, I'll show you."

Owen sighed. "Make it quick. A minute's about all I can spare. I've got a backlog of reports due tomorrow on the system upgrades. You could have called me and I'd have more time for you later in the week."

"Later in the week might be too late."

Blake stood and adjusted his already pristine suit. The guy towered two inches taller than Owen's six-foot-two and never seemed to have a single black hair out of place. Not to mention that icy blue stare of his. The Hurt, as it had been nicknamed by some long-ago family member. That glare was so mighty they should bottle that shit and sell it as terrorist repellent. Back in the day, he and Blake had made good use of The Hurt when scaring off potential suitors from the hot gals they wanted to date themselves. The days before tragedy had struck and Owen had shipped off to fight his country's battles overseas.

The days when they'd both been different men.

Now they were harder, wiser, lonelier...

"Bring Henry along, will you?" Blake said as Owen rounded the desk.

"Fine." He stopped beside the chair and let the iguana climb up his arm to his shoulder, praying to God he didn't relieve himself while up there, then joined Blake in the cramped viewing room where his cousin was busy loading up a section of video from a few days prior.

Onscreen, a beautiful woman with a headful of deep red curls sat at one of the casino's blackjack tables. Her perfect posture and quirky half-grin set her apart from the other players in an instant. He couldn't seem to stop himself from staring at the graceful way she picked up her cards or swiped a stray lock from her forehead, couldn't stop himself from wondering what color eyes went with such striking hair and pretty features.

Wait. What?

Nope. He gave himself a mental shake. Beautiful women had become the bane of his existence. Most definitely *not* going down that road again. He shuffled his feet and frowned, leaning in closer over Blake's shoulder. "What exactly should I be looking at here?"

"You have a cheater at the Lucky Ace."

Nose scrunched, he squinted at the woman once more. "And you think it's her?"

"Not sure, but something was certainly going on at that table that night. Shelby asked me to go over the intake records. This gal won a lot at Blackjack that evening."

"So?" Owen straightened, not liking the fact a cheater might have taken the house right under his nose. He was one of the best casino security bosses in Vegas. And Blake should damned well know. Hell, he'd taught Owen the ropes. "Maybe it's just a winning streak. Or beginner's luck."

Blake gave him a deadpan stare. "This wasn't a simple winning streak. And that woman is no beginner. Prior to this point, she beat the dealer three hands straight. She knows exactly what she's doing."

Henry dug his little claws into Owen's shoulder as if in agreement.

Owen winced, craving his privacy more than ever. He'd re-watch the footage again after Blake left and decide for himself what was happening. "Maybe. Still, that doesn't automatically mean she's cheating. I'll need to analyze everything before I make any accusations. We could get in a lot of trouble if we're wrong."

Blake pushed to his feet and took Henry back. "Whatever you do, make it fast. If it's not the woman, then you've probably got a dirty dealer or something else is going on. The blackjack tables are logging way too many losses. Either way, she won six more times that night before leaving."

Well, fuck. The odds were always in the house's favor and the only way to sway them that consistently was by nefarious means. He hated cheats and liars almost as much as he hated frauds. And when it happened on the floor of his own casino, he took it as a personal insult.

Owen stood before the monitors in the viewing room long after Blake had gone, staring at the beautiful woman as she laughed and joked with an obese man beside her, and his resolve hardened along with his heart. If this woman thought she was so smart, then it would be his greatest pleasure in the world to prove her wrong.

Nobody made a fool of Owen Rockford.

Not anymore.

OWEN LEANED back in his chair and scrubbed a hand over his face.

Three days he'd been investigating the gal from the tapes and still nothing. No name, no address, and sure as hell no paper trail. She was smart. Too smart to be easily tracked through surveillance tapes. The mystery cheat seemed completely untraceable.

Worse yet, Blake hadn't even scratched the surface of her takes. She'd won a total of eleven times that night in his casino, more than three thousand dollars. Far more than mere luck. But he had no way of knowing how many times she'd done that in the past. He'd only happened across her on a few of the tapes, so he'd only seen her win on a few occasions. Maybe those were the only time she'd won? He had no idea how many times she played at the casino or how many of those times she walked away with money. Given Blake's concern, there was a lot more than just her three thousand dollar win at stake. The only way to know for sure if she was up to something was to track every game she played and the only way to do that was to watch her on the tapes. To look through all of them trying to find her would take weeks, maybe months.

He groaned and pressed the heels of his hands into his tired eyes.

Just another gorgeous woman, out to take me for all I'm worth.

Frustrated in more ways than one, Owen exhaled and stared at the mound of files and ledger sheets in front of him. What he really needed was for her to return to the Lucky Ace, weird as that sounded. That way he could see her in person, watch her in action, catch her in the act.

She was smart. But he was smarter.

Restless, he left his office and headed out onto the casino floor. Whenever he felt antsy, taking a spin around the place always made him feel better, helped him work off some of his tense energy. Besides, there was a slim chance maybe his cheater would be there and, if so, he wanted to be ready.

He sidled through a throng of fresh tourists huddled around the penny slots then headed across the thick plush carpet toward the high-limit tables. Crowds weren't usually his thing, always reminded him of the packed choppers back in Iraq when they headed out on missions, but tonight he had a mission of his own. And nothing got in the way of the job. Nothing.

A small group had formed around one of the black-jack tables near the far corner, mostly young men, all of them whistling and whooping when a player he couldn't quite see yet apparently scored. Suspicion mingled with the adrenaline fizzing in his gut and he veered in their direction.

Someone was winning big. With any luck it would be her.

Owen stopped short after he cleared the jumble of people and his world teetered.

Yep. It *was* her.

And damn if she wasn't even more captivating in person. All fiery curls and porcelain skin and her laugh —dry and husky and seductive as hell. Not to mention that outfit. What would've been conservative on most women, looked like an invitation to sin on her—a sleek, black suit showing off the slight, yet well-rounded curves beneath.

She leaned forward to speak with the dealer, one of their long time employees named Faye, and crossed her legs, causing her skirt to rise higher up her slim thigh and show off an impressive array of creamy skin. As if sensing his stare, the woman turned and met his gaze and it slammed into him like a rifle butt to the stomach.

Green. Her eyes were green, pale as jade and twice as exquisite.

ALISON TURNED BACK to the table and the cards in her hand.

Shit. Just shit.

He was seriously the best looking man she'd ever seen.

And he was off-limits. So completely off-limits she'd need an atlas just to find a way to him. *Figures.* She took a deep breath and focused on the game. Men were most definitely not part of her equation these days. She had far too many other problems clambering for her attention.

Like the player next to her and what cards he held. The guy had been flirting with her all night, giving her serious side-eye, accidentally brushing up against her when he'd reach for his drink. All the come-on signs she usually ignored. Hell, he'd even scooted closer to her while she'd been staring at the hunk in the distance.

She re-crossed her legs in the opposite direction, away from him, and glanced up at Faye. With the table full, there wasn't time for their normal banter tonight. Still, her friend gave her a pointed look and tilted her head to the side.

"Rockford McHottie, two o'clock."

"What?" Alison frowned.

"The cutie I've been telling you about," Faye said under her breath. "Over there."

Yeah, I see him.

She didn't dare look again, for more reasons than she

cared to admit. Instead, Alison feigned interest in her cards. "He's all right."

"All right?" Faye snorted. "Girl, you better take some of that cash you won and get some glasses. Trust me. To use your math-speak, you definitely want his hotness tangent to all your curves, sweetie."

Alison chuckled while the guy beside her looked confused, then scared, then moved farther away. *Good.* Faye was one of the few people who got her particular brand of humor and even threw it back in her face on rare occasions. And tonight seemed rare indeed. Without looking, she still felt the weight of the stare heavy on her back. It was enough to give a girl hot flashes, or night sweats. Or both.

To distract herself from her overheated, totally inappropriate fantasies, Alison played along, keeping up the math banter. "So you're saying he could plug his solution into your equation any day, huh?"

"Damn straight, girl." Faye winked. "Not just mine though. I see him measuring your angle. He thinks you're acute-y."

"Ugh." She couldn't restrain her eye roll. "Bad. Really, really bad. Almost as bad as 'He's one well-defined function'."

"Oh." Faye shook her head and laughed. "Yeah. Awful. Okay, okay. You win. I'm done with the math jokes."

Grinning, Alison couldn't resist one more. "I don't

know if he's in my range, but I'd like to bring him back to my domain."

"Really?" Faye's expression shifted from teasing to serious. "Honestly, though. If you really want to meet him, I'll introduce you."

"What? No." Alison held up her free hand. "I was kidding. You know I'm not interested in dating anyone right now. Period."

"I don't know, Al. He's a great guy. I've worked with him for years. Maybe it's time you started putting yourself out there a little more."

"I'm out far enough, okay?" She lowered her voice and glanced around at the other people at the table before looking back at Faye. "Drop it, all right?"

"Fine." Faye called for bets before starting a new deal. "*I'll* drop it."

"What's that supposed to—"

The guy who'd been ogling her all night walked away and a new body slid onto the stool beside her. *Oh shit, oh shit, oh shit.* She struggled to keep her breathing steady and even. Owen Rockford.

Stay calm. Stay. Calm.

He has no idea who I am, what I've been through…

Pulse pounding loud in her ears, Alison kept her attention zeroed on her new cards. Fingers shaking, she tapped the table to request a card from Faye, all of her crystal clear calculations gone straight out the window because of her new neighbor.

"Am I dealing you in, Mr. Rockford?" Faye asked, her tone pure professional politeness.

"No, Faye. I'm on the clock." His deep voice sent an involuntary shiver down Alison's spine. "What's your name?"

Get control of this situation before it controls you.

She took a deep breath. "Can't you come up with a better pick up line than that?"

Faye chuckled. "You should ask her sine."

Alison gave her friend a scathing look.

Not funny. Not funny at all.

Unfazed, Faye grinned, turning her attention to the other players at the table.

"It wasn't a line," Owen said, picking up the thread of their conversation.

Unaccountably frazzled, Alison placed her cards down and scowled at him. "Let me save you some time, okay? I'm not interested."

"Me either." He folded his hands atop the black felt of the table. "But I still need to have your name, if you want to keep playing in my casino."

"You want my name? Fine." She reached into the pocket of her black jacket and pulled out the bogus player's club card she stashed there for these types of emergencies, except it was gone.

Damn. I must've left it back at the apartment.

She refused to risk him recognizing one of her fake IDs, so she went for the helpless female act and a fake smile instead. "Sorry. I must've left my players card at home."

"Ask for her cell number," Faye suggested helpfully.

Not.

Owen watched her with a narrowed, steely glare and she gave as good as she got. Then, so fast she might've missed it, something else flickered in the depths of his brown eyes.

Not annoyance. Not suspicion. Attraction.

Her already erratic heartbeat went haywire.

Alison looked away quick, afraid he might glimpse the same emotion in her stare.

Time to go.

She stood and gathered her chips with all the dignity of a queen. "Then I suppose I won't play in your casino anymore this evening."

"Hang on, Chica," Faye said. "You haven't finished this hand."

The turn of the card revealed the Queen of Hearts.

With Alison's King and Ace, that gave her twenty-one.

Well, shit.

She glanced up at Owen Rockford once more and saw him frowning down at her winning hand.

Right. Most definitely time to go.

Alison snatched up her new winnings, shoved them in her purse and fled from the table as if the hounds of hell were hot on her heels. Given the harsh sound of

Owen's voice as he called after her, they very well could've been.

She'd always believed in luck.

Tonight, however, it seemed her luck had just run out.

OWEN SAT ON HIS STOOL, arms crossed and brow furrowed. "Anything you want to tell me?"

"No." Faye cleared the table from the last hand. "Why?"

He arched a brow, silent.

"You mean her?" Faye cocked her head toward the direction where the woman had just fled. "Sorry. She's not usually like that."

"You know her pretty well then?"

Faye met his eyes. "Am I in trouble, Mr. Rockford?"

He slid her "Closed" sign into the center of the table and gestured for Faye to follow him. "I think we should talk. In my office."

Her tone defeated, she followed him. "Yes, Mr. Rockford."

He couldn't imagine Faye being involved in her friend's scheme. Hell, she'd worked at the Lucky Ace for years, had seniority and benefits. It would be stupid for her to jeopardize all that for a lousy swindle. Still, she had information on the gorgeous cheat.

Information he intended to get.

They stopped outside his office door while he swiped his key. The minute he opened the door however, Peaches rushed out, tackling him to the wall with slobbery dog kisses. *Damn.* He'd forgotten about Shelby dropping the dog off. He pushed Peaches off and took a hold of her collar, grumbling. "This day just keeps getting better and better."

Chuckling, Faye knelt to pet the dog. "What do you mean? She's adorable."

"Take her home, if you want."

"Can't." Faye laughed as Peaches showered her with kisses too. "My landlord doesn't allow pets.'

"Hmm." He led the dog and Faye inside his office then shut the door. "Have a seat."

"Thanks." She took one of the chairs in front of his desk while he took a seat behind it. The dog trotted over and made herself comfortable on a towel Shelby had apparently left behind. "So."

"So." Faye glanced over at Peaches, who stared at Owen with pure puppy love. "Aw. I hope you two will be very happy together."

"Funny. Listen, don't start with me, all right? This is serious, Faye. From where I'm sitting, it looks like you're in cahoots with a felon."

"Excuse me?" She wrinkled her nose. "You mean Alison? No way. She's not a felon."

"How do you know?"

"Because she's not."

Peaches whined and he made the mistake of glancing over and next thing he knew, Owen had a lap full of drooling dog and a persistent paw batting his leg for attention. Not exactly helpful toward the 'stern boss' look he was going for. "How well do you know this Alison?"

"Well enough."

"What's her full name?"

"Alison James."

"She live here in Vegas?"

"Yes."

"Age?'

"Twenty-eight." Faye frowned. "What exactly are you accusing me of, Mr. Rockford?"

"You? Nothing. Yet."

"But you think my friend's done something wrong?"

"I'm not sure."

"I see." From her now prickly demeanor, she didn't appreciate his inquires. "I don't like this line of questioning. I'm not a rat, and I don't feel comfortable handing out other people's personal information. If you want details, I suggest you contact Alison directly."

He was about to tell her that was exactly what he'd like to do, but his cell phone started buzzing in his pocket.

"Hold on." Cursing, he held up a finger while he pulled it out and saw Shelby's photo. *Great.* This dog was about to drive him crazy and they hadn't even spent one full night together. "Tell me you're still here at the casino."

"Hello to you too, Owen," Shelby said, all sunshine and snark.

"Shelby..." He put all the dire warning he could muster into his tone, not easy with a persistent mutt growling for his attention. "Look, I need you to come get Peaches. I know I said I'd try it for a couple of days, but I don't think this is going to work out."

"What? Why not? Seriously, Owen, you can't just return her like a pair of bowling shoes."

"She's interfering with my work. I'm trying to have a serious discussion with an employee and she won't stop bugging me for attention." As if on cue, Peaches batted him once more, this time hard on the thigh and narrowly missing a very important, very sensitive spot. Owen caught her paw and kept ahold, giving the pooch a dark glower. "No. Bad girl."

Shelby continued, unaware. "I left a towel. If she's misbehaving, order her back to it. She's very obedient."

He tried and failed. Peaches remained steadfastly at his feet.

"Please. I really can't right now."

"Fine." Shelby sighed. "I'm at the shelter, but I'll come all the way back and get her if you really can't take her right now. I'm not shredding your paperwork though. This is only a temporary hold. I still think you guys would be great for each other and I plan to have you try this again later. Agreed?"

Resigned, he hung his head. "Agreed."

"I'll be there in twenty minutes."

Owen hung up and stared down at a now quiet and forlorn-looking Peaches. "I'm sorry, okay? It's not you, it's me."

Faye snorted from across the desk. "I've heard that one before too, girl. Don't buy it for a second. Look, can I go now, Mr. Rockford?"

From her belligerent expression, he'd gotten about all he'd get from Faye tonight. "Fine. But I will be investigating your friend, *and* her spontaneous winning streak."

"She's not cheating. I would know if she was and I wouldn't be friends with any cheat. But she's a math whiz." Faye tapped the side of her head. "She's smarter than most, so plays better than most."

Owen's eyes narrowed. "Card counting?" Counting cards in your head wasn't illegal, but it gave players a distinct advantage and was highly discouraged in the casino.

Faye shrugged. "I don't know what she's doing. You'd have to ask her yourself."

Faye left without another word and Peaches whacked him on the leg again, looking toward the door then him again.

"What is it now, huh? You need to go out?"

The dog stood up and danced around excitedly.

"Okay." He grabbed the leash Shelby had left on the desk and clipped it to Peaches' collar. "All right, girl. Let's do this so I can get back to work."

They ducked out of the office and headed through the back service halls to the side employee entrance and the alleyway beyond. There, the dog tugged him down the dark street to the employee parking lot and a patch of grass. While she relieved herself, Owen looked around absently, his mind busy trying to figure out how he could find out more about his crafty new cheater, Alison James.

Beneath the orange glow of a streetlight in the distance, a figure seated on a bench near the bus hut caught his attention. A figure with long red curls tied back in a ponytail and a form-hugging black suit.

Her. It's her.

While he watched, Alison pulled a manila envelope from beneath the bench and tucked it inside her jacket.

His breath hitched, caught, rushed out in a loud exhale.

Damn.

Seems his sexy little cheater had a whole lot more going on than just counting cards.

ALISON PRESSED the envelope tighter to her side and stared straight ahead at the busy street in front of her. She still couldn't shake the feeling she was being watched, even though she'd left her handsome henchman back inside the casino. The knowing look in his warm brown eyes had indicated he had far more information about her than he let on and that scared her more than she could say.

Was he working for the people she was running from? Did he discover what happened in her past?

No. How could he?

She sighed and crossed her legs. She was being ridiculous. There was no way a casino boss like Owen Rockford would have access to that kind of top-secret information.

Still, he suspected she was up to something. Something bad.

On edge, she decided to walk instead of waiting for the next bus back to her apartment.

As the distance between herself and The Lucky Ace increased, the knots of tension between her shoulder blades eased. Several blocks away and after a quick glance around to make sure she wasn't being followed, she slipped the envelope from inside her jacket once more and ripped open the top. Inside was a single folded sheet of paper with a message typed across it. The message was chatty, friendly. If anyone read it they would think it was a message from one friend to another catching up on daily life. But to Alison, it was much more than that. Skimming it, she searched for the secret words of warning:

It's sunny in Seattle.

Nothing. Not a mention of Seattle or the weather at all.

Good.

Her stiff posture relaxed as she tore the letter into pieces and tossed it in a nearby trashcan then continued on home. She was still safe. The past hadn't caught up with her.

Yet.

No doubt it would someday though. How could it not? Not with billions of pharmaceutical dollars on the line, not to mention patient's lives. All because of one error. An error she'd discovered and taken to her boss at Copernatech, only to find her concerns dismissed.

She waited at the corner for the light to change, hiding in plain sight amidst the tourists and partiers out for a good time. Maybe she should never have gone to that reporter with the information—information that would've brought Copernatech to its knees. Thinking back, it probably hadn't been her smartest move, but she couldn't let all those innocent people die because of a mathematical mistake.

No. This way, only one person had died so far. The reporter. A suicide, the coroner had ruled, but Alison knew better. That hadn't been a suicide, that had been murder.

Murder by a pharmaceutical company that would do anything to remain profitable.

So much for her extraordinary math skills earning her a good living. Instead they'd been the reason she'd found the error in the first place—most people wouldn't have had the expertise to catch it—and *that* had almost cost her her life. Still might, if she wasn't careful.

"Excuse me. Sorry." A tourist jostled her in their haste to cross the street, jarring her from her thoughts. She hustled across Las Vegas Boulevard along with the rest of the crowd then headed south toward the basement apartment she rented from her kindly little old landlady, Ms. Baker.

Alison took one last look back at the flashing neon lights of the Fremont Street Experience as she left. This sure as hell wasn't where she'd pictured herself in five years. Back before Copernatech, she'd planned to get a secure job, buy a house of her own, find a good man and get married.

Now?

She snorted and kept moving, focusing on the sidewalk beneath her feet. Well, now she just kept running, kept hiding, kept avoiding detection to stay alive for as long as she could. After the drug company had broken into her place and stolen her research, she knew there was nowhere safe to hide, no one safe in which to confide. Her life these days had become an endless blur of temporary havens, temporary people, temporary lies.

A niggle of unease bored into her newfound relaxation.

Maybe I've stayed here too long. Maybe it's time I moved on again.

Her pulse beat in time with her footsteps as the crowds thinned and residential lawns and fenced in yards took over. Birds called in the cool night air and the smell of fresh-cut grass and fertilizer tickled her nose. Honestly, she'd stayed here longer than anywhere else in the past eighteen months, hoping to build a nice nest egg for herself with her gambling winnings, something to sustain her when the time came for going seriously underground. Unfortunately, after what had happened tonight at the Lucky Ace, she was starting to think it might be time to skip town again.

Unexpected sadness welled at the thought of leaving the only friend she had these days.

Faye Wagner.

Always bubbly, always happy, always there to lend support.

Scowling, Alison crossed the final street and headed toward a non-descript beige house near the far corner of the cul-de-sac. Staying would only endanger both of them. If it was truly time to go, then she needed to do it. Fast and furious, like ripping off a bandage. It would take her a few days, maybe a week, to settle all of her affairs here and erase any tracks she might have inadvertently left behind, then yeah.

Time to go.

Definitely.

Thankfully, at least according to Caroline Biggs—her contact inside Copernatech and the sender of the letter—she still had time to spare.

3

Five days later, Owen sat in the viewing room of his office going over the security tapes from the past week for at least the trillionth time. He'd need a new set of bionic eyes after watching all this crap over and over again, not to mention a lobotomy.

Alison James had been up to something the night he'd met her at the casino. All of his military-trained instincts screamed there was more to her than met the eye. But if she was a cheater, as Blake claimed, she sure as hell wasn't very good at it. At least not based on what he'd seen on tape.

Exhaling loud, he scrubbed a hand over his face and went over the payout reports again. Sure, she'd won several times, more than most, but never in large amounts. He flipped a couple of pages ahead and scanned the columns of numbers. Or maybe his figures hadn't captured all the tables she'd played at either.

And then there was that business with the envelope under the bench. Did that have something to do with the casino cheating? Was she part of some sort of ring that communicated with notes under public benches? He supposed it was possible. There had to be more to the cheating, because from what he could tell Alison wasn't winning the kind of money that Blake had indicated the casino was being cheated out of.

Head aching and vision blurry, he set the spreadsheets aside again an hour later. God, he hated math more than root canals. Still, the answers lurked somewhere in these tallies and totals. Pressing on his throbbing temples to relieve the pain, he closed his eyes and slumped back in his chair. What he needed was a resident egghead to handle all these calculations, someone who lived and breathed equations, someone to help him discern the identity of the real culprit.

His phone buzzed on the desktop and he squinted an eye open to see a picture of Peaches' goofy grin, her tongue lolling out of one side of her mouth, and a message, courtesy of Shelby:

I MISS YOU.

Shit.

He swiped the message away to dismiss it. A pet was

yet another thing he couldn't deal with at present. Having Peaches would only distract him from his work and right now, his work was what kept him sane, kept him going.

Speaking of work...

He sat forward and grabbed the phone, punching Blake's speed dial button.

"Any luck finding out more information on Alison?" he asked once Blake answered.

"Do you have any idea how many people are named Alison James in Nevada? I sure as hell didn't, until now." Blake made some indecipherable sounds that Owen could only hope were directed toward Blake's constant companion, Henry, before continuing their conversation. "If you want me to find out anything useful, I'll need more than her name. Birth date, hometown, something."

"Damn." Owen rubbed his eyes. "Don't have any of that."

"Great." Blake's flat tone inferred the opposite. "Well, I'll keep looking, but it'll be difficult. And what the hell is up with having me put guards on a bus hut bench? Way to waste man hours, bud."

"It's not a waste, all right?" Owen sighed and sat forward. "The other night when I went out to walk Peaches I saw Alison there. She grabbed an envelope from underneath the bench. It must be some kind of drop off point. Not sure how frequently it's used or even what it's used for. Hell, maybe it was only a one-time thing." He scowled, realizing how absurd the whole thing must sound. "I just have this feeling it's worth doing some surveillance, okay?"

"Who's Peaches?"

"What?"

"Peaches. Sounds like a stripper." Owen could feel The Hurt through the phone line. "Are you dating a stripper? Because I've warned you about this shit and—"

"Hell, no. I'm not dating anyone, all right? It's this temporary adoption thing Shelby wanted me to try, but I'm not doing it anymore. Not right now anyway."

"Peaches is a thing?"

"Forget it."

"Fine. Whatever." Blake's suspicious tone was soon replaced by sarcasm. "Anything else I can help you with tonight?"

"Yeah, you can send over a frigging math whiz to help me crunch these damned pay out numbers."

"You're a casino. Don't you already have accountants to do that?"

Owen inhaled slowly, more to keep from punching a hole through his desk, Hulk-style, at his cousin throwing his own words back in his face. *Smartass.* "Yes. We do. But I need fresh eyes on this. Pretty sure my own are ready to bleed from looking at these damned reports all night. Like you said before, sometimes people get lucky. But those lucky people usually end up dumping the money right back into the casino's coffers, or they'll load it onto their player's card or take half in payout or something. Whoever's been taking the house these past couple of weeks hoarded their chips then cashed them—no re-spending, no player's club. My instincts tell me it could be the same cheater. And maybe that's Alison, and maybe it's not."

"Have you seen any other suspicious activity on the videos?"

"Nope. But Alison hasn't been back since I confronted her last week and believe me, I've kept an eye out."

"Hmm." Blake babbled to his lizard pal again, and Owen couldn't help but snicker. Seems the guy had gone head over heels for his new iguana pal. "Then I guess it's lucky for you I happen to know where she is right now, huh?"

"Alison?" Owen straightened. "Where?"

"I have it from a reliable source she stepped into the Golden Summit Gym near Orleans Square about twenty minutes ago."

KICK, *kick, jab, punch.*

Over and over, Alison repeated her karate kata on a heavy bag hung from the ceiling. She'd earned her blue belt for self-defense, so this was both good practice and a good workout. Double win. Plus, it was a good stress reliever too. Well, most of the time anyway.

Today, though, she just couldn't shake the feeling of still being stalked. She bowed then stepped back, allowing someone else the opportunity to practice while she swiped a complimentary towel over the back of her sweaty, tingling neck. She glanced to one side. No one watching her. Glanced to the other side, out the front windows of the gym, and spotted a now familiar figure silhouetted by the bright sunshine.

Owen Rockford.

Her heart skipped then raced in triple speed.

In another time, another place, his presence might have been welcome. Now, though, he only spelled imminent danger.

Is he following me? Is Copernatech close behind?

Shit.

Blood hot and adrenaline surging, Alison moved slowly toward the ladies' locker room, doing her best not to draw attention to herself or her movements. Luckily, he hadn't seen her. She needed to change, needed to squeeze out of the window near the top of the last ladies' shower stall and head home to pack what few belongings she had left.

Whoever the hell Owen Rockford truly worked for, he'd gotten too close.

Which meant her time to escape had officially ended.

4

———

Later that afternoon, with her bag packed and stashed in a locker at the Amtrak station, Alison lingered outside the Lucky Ace's side entrance one last time. Coming here again was a risk, but she couldn't bring herself to leave without saying goodbye to Faye. Friends were a rare luxury these days and Faye had been beyond great. Of course, she'd tried her apartment and even texted first, hoping to catch Faye before her shift, but no luck. So, here Alison stood, with her whole life on the line, gambling everything for one last goodbye.

After a deep breath for courage, Alison stepped inside and tugged the brim of her dark baseball hat lower over her eyes to conceal her face. Head lowered, she made a beeline for the gaming tables, narrowly avoiding a collision with a group of rowdy senior citizens who'd apparently won big on the quarter slots.

Hunched inside her oversized black windbreaker, Alison glanced up over the zipped-up collar and spotted Faye working her usual blackjack table about ten feet away. She waited until the last patron moved to an adjacent table, then hurried over to grab Faye by the arm and pull her aside.

"Hey, I'm working here," Faye said, shaking off Alison's grip. "What's up? And why are you dressed like the Unabomber?"

Alison looked around quickly. "Sorry, I don't have time to explain, but I'm leaving."

"Leaving? To go where?" Faye's voice sounded abnormally loud in the quiet alcove.

"Shhh." Alison stepped closer, her brows furrowed. "I can't tell you, but I wanted to say goodbye."

"Okay, seriously." Faye scrunched her nose "You need to cut the superspy crap, Al. What the hell is going on? You can't just leave Vegas."

"I can and I am. I can't stay here anymore."

Her friend watched her for a moment, eyes narrowed, before the color drained from her cheeks. "Oh, my God. You *are* serious, aren't you?" Faye pulled her behind a nearby copse of potted ferns. "Alison, I know there's something in your past you've kept hidden and whatever it is, it must be bad. I'm okay with you not telling me if you don't want to, but running won't help. Please stay and let me help you, if I can."

Touched by the offer, tears of gratitude welled in

Alison's eyes before she blinked them away. It was tempting. Oh so very tempting, but she couldn't. It wasn't fair to pull anyone else into this murderous mess. "I appreciate it, Faye. More than I can say, but I can't. I won't put you in that kind of danger. I have to go."

"Why? Why now?"

"Someone's following me."

"Who?"

She hesitated. "Your Mr. Hottie McBody."

"Owen?" Faye scoffed. "He's harmless."

"What if he's not though?" Alison rubbed a shaky hand over her forehead. God, she was exhausted. She couldn't remember ever feeling more tired in her life— tired of running, tired of hiding—but she couldn't stop now. Not when her life depended on it. "If he's not harmless and he *is* following me that would explain why he showed up at my gym today."

"Gym? He followed you to the gym?" Faye frowned, then chuckled. "Oh. That's not why he followed you."

"How do you know?"

"Because..." This time, Faye glanced around before speaking. "He pulled me into his office after you bailed the other day. He thinks you're cheating the casino."

"Cheating?"

"Yeah, at Blackjack."

"Oh." *Well, damn.* Alison rankled. What she was doing wasn't cheating. She couldn't help it if she was better at math than most people. Counting cards came as naturally as breathing to a math geek like her, and, while casinos didn't actually like it, it wasn't illegal and certainly *not* cheating if she was using her own God-given skills. "I'm not. Not really."

"I know that." Faye gave her an exasperated look. "And I told him that too, but it's his job to investigate. *That's* why he followed you. I'm sure of it."

Made sense, but it didn't change the fact that Owen looking into her past could only spell trouble for her future. She dug the toe of her black sneaker into the plush carpet. "Look, it honestly doesn't matter why he's doing it. The fact is, he is. I've got secrets. Secrets people are desperate to keep that way. Which means, I still have to leave. Actually, I've stayed too long here as it is. I should've gone a long time ago."

"Okay, fine." Faye reached into the pocket of her uniform vest and pulled out a key. "One more night. Please promise me you'll stay put one more night." She peeked through the ferns at her table and cursed. "The floor manager is lurking around my area again. I have to get back, but go to my place." She grabbed Alison's hand and pressed the key into her palm. "Let yourself in and wait for me. There's food in the fridge and wine on the counter. I'll be home a little after midnight. If you're leaving, then let's say goodbye properly, eh?"

A proper goodbye sounded heavenly at that moment. Plus, her train didn't leave until early the next morning, so she did have hours to kill. Spending them with Faye would make the upcoming months seem less lonely too. She was so tired of being lonely. Reluctantly, she nodded. "Okay. But only for a few hours."

By one the next morning, Alison had watched half a season of *House Hunters International* on Netflix, nibbled her way through two bags of buttered microwave popcorn, and guzzled half of Faye's bottle of wine. She felt antsy and uneasy and was ready to bolt entirely when the sound of her friend's key scraped in the front door lock.

"Hey, girl," Faye said upon entering. She closed the door behind her and relocked it. "Sorry it took me a bit longer to get here with the traffic. Forgot about the fight tonight at the MGM Grand."

Alison swiped the back of her hand across her mouth and crumpled her empty popcorn bag. "No problem. I appreciate you letting me crash here for a couple of hours. I should probably get going though."

She pushed to her feet and headed for the trash can in the kitchen. With all the neon colors beaming from Faye's artwork and furnishing, the place practically glowed in the dark. Not exactly Alison's more neutral and homey style, but it suited her vibrant friend to a T. "Thanks again for the hospitality."

"Nope." Faye stepped forward and blocked her path.

"Not yet. I said we'd have a proper goodbye and I meant it."

"Right. Okay." Alison shuffled from foot to foot, anxious to be on her way. "There's still wine left."

"Good. But I've got something more in mind."

More? That word never boded well for fugitives. "Honestly, Faye. I really need to get to the Amtrak station and get my stuff and—"

"And nothing." Faye grabbed Alison's arm and pulled her toward the bedroom. "I've got plans for you, girlfriend."

She tried to pull free, but her friend's grip was too strong. "Faye, I really can't."

"Like hell. What happens in Vegas, stays in Vegas, right?" She winked then pulled open her closet doors with her free hand and frowned. "Most of my stuff's too big for you, but there must be something in here we can make work."

"Work for what?"

Faye glanced back, her smile devious. "For Glam, of course."

"Glam?" The high-profile karaoke bar was the last place Alison ought to be tonight. "No. Way."

"C'mon." Faye let Alison go and crossed her arms. "What are you, chicken?"

"No. I'm smart. Why the hell would I go to a club with people looking for me?"

"Why not? They say the best place to hide is in plain

sight." Faye looked in her closet again then pulled out a royal blue wrap dress and tossed it at Alison. "Try that."

"I'm not trying anything." She tossed the dress on the bed and headed for the front door. "I really need to go. Goodbye, Faye. Thanks for everything. I'll never forget it."

"Not so fast, girlfriend. You owe me."

Alison squeezed her eyes shut, her hand on the front door handle. Faye was right. She did owe her. For everything from friendship to rent money during the first few months when she'd run short. Too bad the debt was more than Alison could ever repay. "Please don't ask me to do this."

"Already did. You deserve one night out on the town, a little fun in your dreary life. Let me give you that as your going away present. I'll even make sure you arrive at the station in plenty of time to catch your train, okay?"

Much as Alison hated to admit it, it had been far too long since she'd had any fun, time to just act her age instead of having to always be on guard, older, wiser. Faye was right, it would be so awesome to have a few hours as a young, carefree twenty-eight-year-old who sucked at singing and loved to dance again. After all, a few hours wouldn't hurt anything, right?

"Okay."

5

———

Twelve-fifteen a.m. God, how long have I been staring at these figures?

Owen blinked fast to ease his eye strain. So far, he'd gone over all the stats for the individual games and yeah, Blackjack showed a higher than usual payout, but then again, so did poker, craps, and the slots. Which meant his late-night accounting session had netted exactly squat when it came to useful intel on his cheater issues.

He sighed and leaned back in his chair, stretching his stiff shoulders and neck and tossing his pencil on the desk. Alison James was hiding something. Had to be. Now, if only he knew what the hell it was.

She hadn't been back to the casino and he'd never seen her at the gym Blake had sent him to. Maybe she'd skipped town. That would be good. Then he wouldn't have to deal with her in person and the less

Owen had to deal with her in person, the better off he was. Owen had a feeling that dealing with Alison James in person could be dangerous … and not just to the casino.

"Any luck?" Blake leaned against the frame of Owen's open office door, sans lizard. "With the cheater, I mean."

"None." Owen yawned. "Where's your friend?"

"I took Henry home a few hours ago. He needed his beauty rest."

"Got that right." He chuckled then shook his head. "The only person Alison James seems to have contact with here is one of my dealers, gal by the name of Faye Wagner. But I've already spoken with her too and got nothing."

"Hmm." Blake straightened and checked his watch. "What time does her shift end?"

"Midnight. About fifteen minutes ago."

"Want me to see if I can catch her? Maybe she'll let something slip you missed. After all, I am known for my charm and persuasion."

He waggled his brows and Owen snorted. "Try if you want. Good luck catching her before she leaves though. Most of the dealers can't wait to get home after their late shifts."

"I'm on it."

Blake gave him a thumbs-up then disappeared down the hall while Owen went back to his numbers. The next time he glanced up again, another forty-five minutes had passed and he was pretty damned sure he'd be permanently cross-eyed from staring at numbers all night long.

Work comp covered that, right?

"Hey," Blake said, poking his head around the door again.

"Hey. You catch Faye?"

"Nope. Already gone. I spoke to a couple of the other dealers instead. Didn't find out anything new though. Sorry." Blake took a seat in front of Owen's desk. For once, the guy actually looked tired, with dark shadows below his icy blue eyes. "Want to grab a beer or something on the way home?"

"Aw, man, I'd love to," Owen said, meaning it. "But I can't. Still got to find something useful in these numbers. Whoever this cheater is, they're taking us for a metric shit ton of cash. Shelby will have my ass if I don't put a stop to it soon."

"According to my calculations, you've already put in well over sixty hours this week. The reason I know this because in addition to our other fine services, Rockford Security also handles the payroll for the casino." Owen glanced up and Blake gave him a cool smile. "Signed your paycheck myself, cuz, and your overtime borders on criminal."

"I know." Owen raked a hand through his short, brown hair. "Believe me, Shelby's been on me about that too. Can't be helped though. All those extra hours are necessary if I'm going to find this crook."

"This is personal for you, isn't it?"

"Damn straight."

Blake gave a curt nod. "Well, trust me on this. Whoever this cheater is, they'll wait until tomorrow." He pushed to his feet and straightened his suit jacket, a glint of mischief returning to his eyes. "Now, are you coming with me to the bar or do I have to drag you?"

"Drag me?" Owen scoffed. "Good luck with that."

"I might've left the force for a few years, but I could still kick your ex-Marine ass, bud. In fact, if I remember right, I've kicked your ass many times over the years. Want me to do it again tonight?"

His tone was amused, but his expression was pure determination. Owen knew that look, all too well. It was the same look that all the Rockfords got when they had an idea and intended to see it through no matter what. Hell, it was the same look he saw in his own mirror every morning before he headed to the casino.

Looked like he'd be getting a drink whether he wanted one or not.

Resigned, Owen pushed to his feet and grabbed his jacket off the back of his desk chair. "Fine. But just a quick beer. If I'm leaving early, I want to at least try to get some extra sleep."

"Okay. How's your new dog, by the way. What was her name? Pickles?"

"Peaches. And she's not my dog. She's one of the rescues at Shelby's shelter and she's trying to match me up with her." They headed out of the office and Owen secured the door behind them before following Blake down the marble hallway and out onto the casino floor. "She wanted me to take the dog home this past weekend for a trial run, but things didn't work out. Where are we going anyway? And please don't say the Lucky Ace bar."

"Nope. Thought we'd try a place a couple of blocks from here. It's within walking distance of the Rockford offices. I've been there a couple of times after work." They headed out into the bustling night and stood at the corner, waiting for the light to change. "I think it's a good idea."

"What?"

"You having a dog. Henry's made all the difference for me. I never thought I'd have time to spare, but it works."

Owen contemplated the idea the rest of the way to the bar. Shelby sent him even more pictures of Peaches, each with a funny little message or emoji attached. Much as he hated to admit it, he was starting to like them. Hell, earlier today he'd even found himself checking his phone to see if a new one had come in.

Maybe Blake was right. Maybe having a dog, someone more than himself to care for, would be good. As they stepped up to the door of a place called Glam— all neon bright lights and black painted windows—he stopped and scowled. "This is where we're going?"

"Yep." Blake smiled blandly and opened the door. "It's fun. You'll see."

"It's karaoke."

"So?"

"So, I don't sing."

"Neither do I. I come to watch the other people." Blake led him across a packed room and over to two empty stools at the bar. "Order whatever you want. My treat."

They gave the bartender their ale choices as a new duet started on stage. The off-key rendition of an eighties power ballad would've caused paint to peel and Owen covered his ears, laughing. "Jesus, I haven't heard pitiful wailing like that since the war."

"Most of them aren't *that* bad." Blake took a swig from his bottle then glanced past Owen toward the front door, his smile turning wicked. "Well, look at that. Maybe you'll have a chance to question your favorite little cheater again after all."

Owen followed Blake's pointing finger to two women who'd just arrived.

Faye Wagner and... *Oh, shit!*

He narrowly avoided choking on his beer and narrowed his gaze on his cousin. "What the heck, man? Did you set this up?"

"Me? Nah." Blake scrunched his nose and held up his hands in innocence. "Like I said, your dealer was long gone when I went looking for her. But I will say it again, the ladies can't resist me, man. Is that the Faye in question? If so, I'll be glad to find out what she knows."

"Charming my ass. And yeah, it is." Owen gave Blake a disparaging look to go with his scowl. "Henry's more charming than you."

"Smile." Blake nudged him on the shoulder and pointed toward the women again. "Here they come. You wanted to know more about Alison and what she's hiding, right? Here's your chance."

"C'MON." Faye grabbed Alison's arm and tugged her forward. "Let's get something to drink at the bar."

Alison trailed after her, not given much choice with her friend's persistent grip, then halted abruptly when she spotted the two men staring back at them from the bar.

Oh crap. Oh crap. Oh crap.

"Faye. Faye, stop. I can't go up there. Owen's here. You know, the guy who's the reason I'm leaving." She pivoted fast to head for the door again. "I'm out of here."

Faye kept ahold of her arm, however, halting her after two steps. "Calm down, Al. I'm sure he's just here having a drink. He's not going to arrest you or anything."

"Yeah?" Anger welled inside her. "What if he does! What if he … hey wait a minute. Did you set this up?"

"No, really. I had no idea he was going to be here. I

swear." Faye pulled her closer and whispered. "Act normal, okay, and everything will be fine."

Act normal? Easy for Faye to say.

I hate lying. I've never been a good liar.

No wonder Copernatech finally caught me.

"Let's go." Faye tugged her forward again. "Looks like a couple of stools opened up."

"Who's the other guy?" Alison asked, her gaze locked on Owen.

"His name's Blake Rockford," Faye said, maneuvering them through the throngs of partiers. "He owns Rockford Security. Another McHottie, if you ask me."

Great. As if one snooping guy wasn't enough, now she had two Rockfords poking their noses into her private, personal past.

What if they see through my disguise? What if they expose my secrets? What if...

She smoothed her hand down the front of the royal blue wrap dress. Not her usual conservative style, by any means. Far too low-cut and curve hugging for her taste. Faye had insisted on doing her hair and makeup too, teasing and primping her to within an inch of her life. If she was leaving this life behind, Faye had insisted, she might as well do it in style.

Now, though, as Alison looked at Owen Rockford, Alison felt way more vulnerable than she ever had before. From the strong set to his shoulders to the spark of fire in his warm brown eyes, Owen Rockford looked like a force of nature. A force she wasn't sure she should tangle with.

Faye glanced back at her and frowned. "Relax. You look like you're headed for a firing squad."

Sudden irritation fired Alison's blood, dissolving some of her fear. "How am I supposed to relax? I tell you this guy's following me and what do you do? You force me to talk to him. For all I know, he's a psycho stalker."

"He's not a stalker." Faye stopped and faced her once more, only feet away from the two men. She placed her hands on Alison's shoulders and looked her directly in the eye, her voice calm. "Listen to me. This is all a big misunderstanding. Talk to him. Tell him the truth and let him see the wonderful, smart, beautiful woman I love. He'll realize you're not the cheater he's looking for and all will be well, okay? Maybe you'll even realize that you can stay after all."

Like life's ever that easy.

As if sensing Alison's reluctance, Faye changed tactics. "One drink. We'll have one drink and if you're still uncomfortable, then we'll leave and I'll go wait at the train station with you. Deal?"

Alison knew better than to argue with Faye when she had her mind set on something. "Fine. One drink. That's it."

"Perfect." Faye tugged Alison to the bar and ordered them both a Hurricane before turning her attention to the Rockford men. "Hello, Mr. Rockford. And Mr. Rockford. Fancy seeing you two here."

"Fancy, huh?" Owen muttered, taking another swig of his beer while watching Alison over the rim. "I've got another word for it."

"Ms. Wagner," Blake said, from over Owen's shoulder, then extended his hand. "We haven't officially met, but Owen filled me in about you. And please call me, Blake."

"Nice to meet you, Blake." Faye shook his hand and batted her eyelashes, in full flirt mode now. Faye took a sip of her drink and smiled. "You sing, Blake? And feel free to call me Faye."

"Only when forced, Faye." Blake returned Faye's smile with a polite one of his own, his somewhat stiff demeanor at odds with Faye's overt come-ons. The guy looked several years older than Owen and whatever else might run in the family, the handsome gene was certainly one of them. With his tailored suit and chiseled face, Blake Rockford was all debonair swagger and lethal confidence. Exactly the type Faye went gaga over. Never mind he seemed oblivious to her friend's advances. "Care to move closer to the action, Faye?"

"I'd love to get closer to your action, Blake."

Alison did roll her eyes at that one, shaking her head as she watched her friend bail on her, leaving her alone with Owen. She took a larger than normal sip of her own giant-sized, neon blue Hurricane and wrinkled her nose at the burn in her throat. Deceptively frou-frou and fruity, these suckers packed quite a wallop. Given the fact she'd only had popcorn for dinner, she'd be on her ass in no time flat if she kept this up.

She glanced over to find Owen Rockford still watching her, his expression stoic, though a small muscle ticked near his tense jaw. Apparently, he wasn't as relaxed as he wanted her to believe either.

When in doubt, revert to math.

Math was straight-forward. Math didn't lie. Math didn't betray you the way people did.

She tucked a stray red curl behind her ear and grinned. "What did Al Gore play on his guitar?"

Owen remained silent.

"An algorithm." She snorted, loud enough for people closer by to turn and stare at her. Embarrassed heat prickled her cheeks and she stared down at the bar again. So much for small talk. "Get it? Al Gore rhythm. Sorry. That was bad."

"Awful." His voice sounded lower than she remembered. Rougher. "Faye says you're unusually good at math."

Alison shrugged. "I guess I can hold my own."

"Is that why you win so much at cards?"

"I don't cheat if that's what you mean. Math comes naturally to me. It's pretty useful, I bet you use it a lot too Mr. Rockford."

"Owen."

"Okay, Owen. But only if you call me Alison."

"Fine." He took another gulp of beer. "I hate math. Never was good at it. So, I rarely use it."

"I bet you use it all the time and just don't realize it. How many times do you walk into a room at your casino and calculate the number of heads in a crowd to make sure you're not overcapacity? Or watch the tables, guesstimating the probability that someone will prove troublesome?"

"I don't know." Owen tapped on the bar to order another beer. "I prefer listening to my gut versus my brain when it comes to troublesome situations. Not numbers."

"You might not do it consciously." She turned down the bartender's offer for another Hurricane. "But math is still there, lurking in the background. Perhaps if you embraced it, you'd be even better at your job."

"Really?"

"How many people are in the Lucky Ace at any given time? Three hundred? Five hundred? More?" She took another sip of her drink. "For a nice round number, let's say a thousand people. With all those people, what made you single me out as a cheater? Your gut?" When he didn't respond, she smiled. "Sorry, but if you analyzed the data mathematically, you would've seen I lose as much as I win. Hardly an effective strategy, if I had one. I mean, if I was cheating, wouldn't I want to win all the time?"

"Nope." He twisted the cap off his new beer and took a drink. "Not if you're smart."

"I'm flattered."

He stopped mid-sip. "Why?"

"That means you think I'm intelligent. And I am. Just not that kind of intelligent."

The alcohol in her system buzzed through her bloodstream, lifting her inhibitions and flushing her body with warm relaxation. Apparently it was doing the same to him, if the way he swayed slightly toward her was any indication.

"I do think you're smart, Alison." Owen set his beer aside and leaned closer, his warm brown gaze holding hers. "Maybe too smart for your own good."

Warning bells went off and Alison didn't know whether to lean closer to him or run away. Before she could do either, Faye and Blake returned.

"That was so much fun!" Faye's voice was perky. "We should definitely come back here again, Al. You ready to go?"

"Sure," she mumbled, uncertain her shaky legs would carry her as far as the door, let alone all the way to the train station. "Okay."

"Right." Faye helped her off her stool then placed a steadying arm around her waist. "Well, thanks for a fun time, Blake. Owen. See you both later."

They weaved back through the crowd toward the

front door and it wasn't until they were outside again that Faye stopped and leaned Alison against the brick wall of the building. "Are you sure you're fit to travel tonight?"

Alison stared at her friend wondering if Faye had a some sort of plan. Running into the Rockford's tonight couldn't have been a coincidence... could it? But if Faye was planning something it wasn't to hurt Alison. It was to help her. And if Faye didn't think Owen Rockford was a threat, Alison could take that to the bank. But Faye didn't know the real reason why Alison needed too run. Still, the hurricanes were strong and she wasn't used to drinking. Maybe it was smarter to wait until tomorrow.

She'd be out the price of her train ticket, but that seemed a small price to pay for a clear head and a clear plan for her future. "Maybe I should sleep this off at your place then figure out what to do in the morning."

"That's my girl," Faye hailed a cab then took hold of Alison once more. "Sleep it off and things will look different in the morning, I promise."

6

___

Owen walked into his apartment half an hour later and tossed his keys on a side table by the door. He was more conflicted than ever about the casino cheater. His gut told him it wasn't Alison James, but there had been something off about her too.

Alison James was definitely hiding something and that was unacceptable.

After all, his ex Faith had done that too, once upon a time.

Faith...

Jesus. Even five years later the pain was still fresh.

Temples pounding and head swimming with alcohol and memories, Owen clicked on the lights in his bedroom only to find an excited Peaches sitting on the middle of his mattress, tail thumping and goofy dog grin in full force.

"Dammit, Shelby." He dug his phone out of his pocket and speed dialed her number, but it went straight to voicemail.

Shit. A quick glance at his bedside clock showed two-fifteen in the morning. Of course, she'd be in bed by now, like any normal, sane person. He left a terse voicemail and hung up then turned back to Peaches, resigned.

He sank down on the edge of the bed, more exhausted than he could remember, and glanced over at his unexpected canine companion. "You better not snore."

As if in response, Peaches went down on her front paws, hiking her butt in the air with her tail still going. Classic play position. She nuzzled his hand then licked the back of it, whining.

"All right, girl." He couldn't help chuckling at her playful demands for attention and scratched her behind the ears. Peaches rolled over and exposed her belly her expression one of pure ecstasy.

Laughing, he headed into the bathroom where he jammed on the shower and stripped then stepped under the cool spray, grateful for the brisk temperature and the time alone to think about what Alison had said.

What made you single me out as a cheater? Your gut?

Her question continued to swirl in his brain like a cockeyed tilt-a-whirl.

Yeah. My gut. And my cousin, Blake.

Except, over the past couple of days, his gut had

changed sides. Hours and hours of analysis and watching security feeds had him doubting whether she was really the person he was looking for. Oh, she was still hiding secrets, no question. But his prized instincts told him she wasn't ripping off his casino. At least not by herself anyway.

Maybe his thought of her being part of a gambling ring when he'd seen her take the envelope from under the bench wasn't so far-fetched.

He soaped up and scrubbed shampoo into his hair. A ring would explain a lot, actually. Like why she never won very much and why she was still so reluctant to come clean. If she was part of a bigger organization, it was entirely possible she'd been forced into it, coerced against her will. And that would explain the envelope. Instructions for the next take, perhaps?

Who else would be in on it? The dealers? Faye? He hated to think Faye would have anything to do with it, but her table did have a lot of losses and she was chummy with Alison.

Hell yeah, the more he thought about it, the more it made sense.

As he stepped under the spray again to rinse off, the years seemed to trickle away along with the soap and he was back in the Marines once more. Twenty-six and green when it came to women. Oh sure, he'd had plenty of girlfriends, but nothing serious.

Not until Faith.

She'd been the most beautiful woman he'd ever seen in real life and he'd fallen hard and fast. He'd bought into her praise and her seduction hook, line, and sinker. And after she'd satisfied both his body and his youthful ego, she'd plied him for information. Top-secret military information he'd been granted access to because of his rank. Information he'd managed to keep secret, despite her obvious temptation.

Good thing too, considering it had later come out she'd been a North Korean spy and he wasn't the first officer she'd plied with her talents. He'd been investigated, disciplined by the military court, and gotten off lucky with an honorable discharge and no time in the brig for his troubles.

Clean and now most definitely sober, he shut off the water and fumbled for a towel. He dried off fast then stepped out of the shower with the wet towel slung low around his hips. He brushed his teeth and did a quick shave before shutting off the lights and padding over to the bed to slide between the cool sheets at last.

Lights off, he punched his pillow twice then settled in and closed his eyes, Peaches snuggling up on top of the comforter and stretched out lengthwise beside him before snoring loudly.

Perfect. Owen thought as he tried to fall asleep.

Beeeeeeeeppppppp.

One eye squinted open, Owen peered over at the clock on his nightstand. Something warm and heavy lay draped across his chest and the distinct smell of wet fur tickled his nose.

He pushed Peaches off him and back onto her side of the bed then reached over to slam off the alarm. God, it couldn't be six a.m. already. Impossible. It felt like he'd just closed his eyes and...

A wet tongue in his ear jolted him awake.

He shuddered and sat up fast only to come face to face with a panting Peaches. She licked his face in response then danced around excitedly in circles.

Right. Potty time. He got up and pulled on a pair of sweatpants he found in a drawer and his dress shirt from the night before then searched the apartment for the dog's leash and finally found it in the kitchen, alongside a bag of food, a toy, and a note he assumed was from Shelby.

Yeah, he'd be having words with his boss about using the key he'd given her to his apartment for surprise doggy drop-offs, but first he needed to get Peaches outside before she had an accident he didn't want to have to clean up this early.

Twenty minutes later, they returned and he felt a bit more awake after his dawn sojourn. He started a pot of coffee then set out food and water for Peaches before finally taking a good look around his living room.

Well, crap didn't notice any of that last night. Gaze narrowed, he stared at the neat rows of family photos hung on the wall over his sofa.

Apparently Shelby hadn't been the only one invading his space lately.

Seems his cousin Liv had taken it upon herself to do some decorating at his place. The coffeemaker beeped and he fixed himself a mug then went in search of what other damage she'd inflicted. The cabinet beneath the sink had been fully stocked with cleaning supplies. A not so subtle hint about his bachelor status.

Nice. He was clean, if not always tidy.

Next he moved on to the nearby guest half-bath. A large first aid kit hung from one wall. Okay, that might actually be useful, given his culinary skills—or lack thereof. Couldn't fault her for that one.

An hour later, he'd inspected all the other rooms and found no more surprises and still managed to get dressed and ready for work. Stepping back into the kitchen to place his now empty coffee mug in the sink, Owen smiled. Honestly, much as Liv's meddling bugged him, he did appreciate her efforts to make him feel like part of the family again.

"C'mon, girl." He patted his thighs and Peaches scurried over, her nails clacking loud on his hardwood floors. "Ready to see your mommy again?"

Tongue lolling and eyes bright, the dog stood still

while he clipped on her leash again then waited for him to gather up her bowls and food and toy.

"Good, girl." Owen scratched her head on the way out the door. "Let's go find Shelby."

Except once he reached the Lucky Ace, Shelby was nowhere to be found.

Damn. She only came by on designated days, leaving the regular management of the casino to him and a couple of her other most trusted employees. Today wasn't her day. He took Peaches to his office and closed the door behind them then called Shelby on his phone. This time she picked up after the first ring.

"Paws and Play, this is Shelby. How may I help you?"

"You can help me by picking up your dog so I can get to work."

"What are you talking about?" Shelby sounded genuinely surprised.

Owen wasn't buying it for a second. "Stop. Just come get Peaches, okay?"

"Peaches? Seriously, Owen. I have no idea what you're talking about. Peaches was fostered out to someone else yesterday."

"Well, whoever took her decided to drop her off at my place, because she slept in my bed last night."

"Lucky girl."

"Cut the snark and get over here, all right?"

As if in agreement, Peaches barked loud and Shelby snickered.

"Fine. Let me notify her foster first."

Suspicion blended with his annoyance. Whoever had filled out the paperwork obviously had a key to his apartment as well, and there were only two people besides himself with that honor. "Who's the foster?"

He already knew the answer before she said the words. "Liv."

"You know what, I'll call her myself. I've got a few other gifts to thank her for too. This way I can take care of it all with one call. Thanks, Shelby."

Owen ended the call then stared at the dog at his feet.

Marvelous. Now he had two women pushing him toward pet adoption. Three, if you counted the over-enthusiastic Peaches—her expression brimming with please-love-me, gut-wrenching pathetic-ness.

"Looks like you're stuck with me a bit longer, girl." He got out her bowls, filled one with food and the other with a bottle of water from his mini-fridge, then set them off in one corner of his office along with her towel and toy. "Until your Aunty Liv comes to pick you up."

With the dog settled, Owen called Liv, only to get her voicemail.

Christ, aren't any of these people at work when I need them?

Exasperated, he left a message then opened his computer and sorted through his e-mails.

Toward the bottom of the screen he found a new one

from Blake listing three new possibilities for the casino's cheater. There were screenshots of each candidate's face but little other information, though Blake mentioned some new facial recognition software his company was trying out that would alert Owen when any of the new suspects set foot inside the Lucky Ace.

Interesting.

He quickly sorted through the rest of his messages and was ready to close the laptop when a notification dinged. Apparently Blake's new software worked already. The screen text said one of the suspects, Greg Walpole— mid-thirties, stocky build, dark hair, beard—had entered the casino moments earlier.

Time for some hands on investigation.

Adrenaline pumping, Owen pushed to his feet and straightened his suit jacket before heading for the door. Except once he stepped outside, Peaches barked loud and scratched at the door.

Ugh. This is not good for business. Not at all.

Reluctantly, he went back inside and grabbed her leash, clipping it on before leading her out the door. Surprisingly, she stayed at his side, not pulling at all like she usually did but heeling right next to him like a pro.

Together, they headed out onto the casino floor and soon located Walpole at the gaming tables, his dealer clearly under the weather—judging by the guy's constant cough and greenish complexion. Owen and Peaches stuck to the shadows, wanting only to observe and learn the guy's tells, to see if he displayed any cheating types of behavior. Not long after he'd taken up his position, however, in came Faye with a clearly-hungover Alison in tow.

Faye headed directly for Walpole's table and pulled the sick dealer aside before taking his place behind the table. She'd apparently been called in as reinforcement, which was good considering the other dealer looked like he barely had the energy to haul his sick ass home.

The bulk of Owen's attention, though, rested solely on Alison, despite his resolve not to dwell on her any longer. His interest really piqued when she tried to leave the table and Walpole blocked her way. Seeing some stranger, a possible low-life, putting the moves on her sent Owen's protective instincts skyrocketing.

Not to mention she looked like death warmed over, her pale skin shadowed and her pretty green eyes tired and puffy. Despite the warm day, she wore a tee-shirt, black jacket and jeans. She was obviously not feeling well and all this asshole seemed to want to do was bother her. Alison shook her head and stepped away from the guy, but he still persisted.

Even Peaches seemed uneasy as Owen watched the guy reach for Alison again. The guy took her arm and Alison winced and that was enough.

Time to kick some ass.

Before Owen had time to intervene, however, Peaches launched forward, barreling full-tilt straight for

Walpole and Alison. Owen strode behind, feeling every bit as menacing as the dog.

As they approached, Alison's eyes widened and Walpole stepped back, releasing her to raise his arm in defense. "What the fuck is going on? Is that thing rabid?"

Peaches growled low.

"Sit, girl." Owen never took his eyes off the guy for a second as the dog settled obediently at his feet. "She's part of our new casino security. Is there a problem with that, Mr.?"

Expression belligerent, Walpole stormed off moments later without answering.

"Good girl," Owen said, watching as Peaches walked over and nudged Alison's hand. She knelt to pet her, seemingly unafraid despite the dog's earlier display of aggression toward Walpole. "I think she likes you."

Alison looked over at him, silent, before straightening.

Peaches returned to his side and plopped a wallet down at his feet.

Frowning, Owen picked it up and noticed Alison's driver license stuck in the front. Her birthdate was listed, along with her address. He quickly memorized both before handing it back. "Sorry about that. She's still new."

"Right." Alison shoved the wallet back in her jacket pocket then glanced from him to Faye. "I've got to go."

"Heading home?"

Alison nodded. "Yeah."

"See you later then?" Faye asked, her tone hopeful.

Alison glanced at Owen, a slight flush coloring her pretty cheeks, then her gaze shifted to Faye. "Yeah. See you later."

"Great." Faye perked up and grinned at Owen. "How are you this fine day, Mr. Rockford?"

"Good, Faye." Alison left the casino while Peaches batted Owen on the leg, eager for attention. Thanks to his new canine companion, he now had a way to find out more about his mysterious beauty. "Really good, thanks."

As he and Peaches walked back to his office, Owen started to think maybe having the dog around wouldn't be such a bad idea after all.

7

―――――

Later that afternoon, Alison sat in the Greyhound bus station waiting for her ride. She'd quickly repacked all her stuff at Faye's, stopped at her own apartment and left a note for Ms. Baker that she'd gotten a good job opportunity and would be moving and not to worry. She left a check to cover two months' rent mostly because she didn't want to short Ms. Baker, but also in case Copernatech traced her. She wanted to throw them off track and make them think she was still in town. Then she made a beeline for the bus station. Since she'd used—or almost used—the train before, she opted for the bus this time. Even though all signs indicated Copernatech hadn't caught up with her yet, one could never be too careful. She was doing the right thing by leaving now, before they got too close.

She flipped through the pages of the latest celebrity

tabloid and tried to think optimistically about her future, no matter how desolate things seemed at present. Loneliness clung to her like a wet blanket, but she couldn't stay.

Things had gotten far too close for her comfort.

The overhead P.A. system crackled to life and a woman's voice reverberated from the speaker in the corner. "Attention passengers, Bus number two-oh-nine to Dallas/Fort Worth now boarding at platform number six. Thank you."

Alison draped her purse across her body then reached for her duffle, feeling the buzz of her phone inside. Swearing, she pulled it out as she headed toward the exit, then stopped short. Several passengers jostled her while she stared at the screen. The one-word on the first line of the message from Faye chilled her blood:

S.O.S.

NEED HELP AT LUCKY ACE

Crap.

She stepped off to the side, out of the way of the other busy travelers, and scowled. Faye was the closest friend she'd had in a long time, maybe ever. And Faye knew Alison's urgency to get out of town as quick as possible, if needed. She wouldn't send this as a casual joke or a ploy to get her to stay. No. Something was definitely wrong. She scrolled through, but found no other messages from her friend.

Alison quickly ran the probabilities in her head. Owen suspected her of cheating, but no one had given any sign of knowing about her past with Copernatech. And her secret contact had given her the all-clear as far as her cover was concerned. It was fairly safe here still and Faye was the closest thing she'd had to a real friend in a long time.

I'll stay and help Faye because she's right. I owe her. Just this once, I'll stay.

Decision made, she hustled out of the bus station and headed for the line of cabs waiting at the entrance instead. Her top-tier ticket was transferrable to another date—unlike the train ticket where she'd had to eat the cost. Lesson learned. If things went south again, she'd come back and catch the next Greyhound and zoom out of town faster than a roadrunner on speed.

Climbing into the back of a bright yellow taxi, she gave the driver the Lucky Ace's address then slumped back in her seat for the short ride to the casino.

A short time later, the driver swerved to the curb. Alison paid her fare then bustled into the casino and straight for the tables, except... no Faye.

Well, shit.

"Have you seen Faye Wagner?" she asked, stopping one of the other dealers.

"Mr. Rockford took her to see the owners," the guy said, his frown as dark as his tone.

Dread bubbled like toxic sludge through her system.

This job was Faye's life. If she lost it, then... Alison swallowed hard and forced a polite smile, trying to remain calm. "Do you know why?"

"Not sure. Neither of them looked too happy though."

"Thanks." Alison headed for the hallway. Surely he couldn't suspect Faye of any wrongdoing. She'd been a faithful employee at the Lucky Ace for years. She'd never do anything wrong. She was honest and fair and kind and...

"I'm sorry ma'am," a beefy security guard said, blocking her entry. "You can't go back there."

She seriously considered karate kicking him into tomorrow, but given his size and her luck today, he'd probably fall on her and crush her. Reluctantly, Alison started to walk away until the sound of nails scratching on a door echoed down the hall, followed by a distinct canine whine. Alison snorted and glanced back to the guard. "Sounds like someone has to go outside. Better take her out before she makes a mess. I'm sure the owners wouldn't appreciate doggy doo-doo all over their brand new carpeting, huh?"

The guard didn't budge.

Great. Time to come up with another plan.

She slipped into a secluded alcove along the wall behind some slots for privacy to think. From here, she still had a good view of the hall entrance, so when the guard did leave his post several minutes later, she waited with avid interest. Soon, he returned with Owen Rockford's dog in tow. Apparently her suggestion had worked better than she thought.

Smiling, she waited until both the guard and the dog had disappeared outside then headed for the hallway once more. Time was short so she wasted no time and went directly to the office door marked Owen Rockford, Head of Casino Security. Voices drifted out through the heavy wood door. One of them she recognized as Owen's. The other was definitely Faye's, but she couldn't quite hear what they were saying. It sounded like they were inside an inner office. Maybe this door led to a hallway...if she could just get into the hallway, she could hear what was going on...

A keypad glowed from the wall, beside a card reader. Maybe...

Alison exhaled onto the keypad then squinted, making note of the fingerprints. Next, she scanned the numbered keypad to find the most worn digit. Wear indicated the first digit in the sequence, given the user's skin would retain the most oils and erode the ink faster on that key. Finally, based on the fingerprints she'd seen and the first number, six configurations were possible. More than she'd hoped, but it was better than nothing.

Now, if she hurried, she could find the right combination before the guard got back or the in-house IT guys got wise. *Punch, punch, punch. No, no, no.* She made it through three combos and started on a fourth when the door flew open to reveal a decidedly grumpy Owen.

He glanced from the keypad to her, one eyebrow raised. "Most people knock."

Alison straightened and held herself as regally as possible under the circumstances. "Most people issue a warning before they abduct other people's friends."

"Abduct?" His flat tone was the verbal equivalent of an eye-roll. "Faye's hardly kidnapped. She's my employee. I'm questioning her as part of an ongoing security investigation. Fully within my right and the law."

She sent me an S.O.S. Why S.O.S.?

Before she could respond, another female voice called out from inside the office. "Who is it, Owen?"

"No one important."

Owen started to close the door in Alison's face, but she wedged a foot inside to stop him then took advantage of his surprise to squeeze inside. Faye was seated in front of Owen's desk along with another woman she didn't recognize. There was another man in there too, the same height as Owen but lankier and tougher.

Looked like that guy had been through some hard times, just like her.

Faye frowned, nose wrinkled. "Al?"

Summoning her courage and her outrage, Alison crossed her arms and held her ground, the heavy duffle slung over her shoulder making her muscles ache. "What's going on here?"

Mr. Tough Guy moved in front of the strange blonde woman, his protection of her written in every tense line of his body. "Depends on who you are."

"I'm a friend of Faye's."

The blonde shooed her protector out of the way then smiled at Alison. "That must be her. The girl Blake told us about."

Blake Rockford? Alison's heart sank. The only time she'd met Blake Rockford was at Glam, and the'd barely talked. Why had they been talking about her? Oh, right… becasue they all thought she was cheating. Apparently her attempt to convince Owen otherwise hadn't worked. But she wasn't here about herself, she was here for Faye. Determined to stay on track, she pressed onward. "I'll ask nicely one more time. What's going on here?"

Owen brushed past her. "As you know, we have a cheater in the casino and Faye might have information about this mystery crook's identity."

"That's ridiculous." Alison tossed her long red curls over her shoulder. "How would Faye know anything? She's the most honest person I've ever met."

"Honest. Really?" Owen snorted and sank back into his seat behind the desk. "That's funny, coming from you. You wouldn't know honest if it bit you on the ass. In fact, I've got plenty of clues *you're* the cheater we're looking for."

"God, are we back to that again?" She placed her hands on her hips, her nerves overtaken by annoyance. "Let me say it for you again. Slower this time, so you'll catch on. I'm. Not. A. Cheater."

Silence.

Four gazes remained locked on Alison as if expecting a show.

Fine. They wanted a show? Fine. She'd sure as hell give them one, for Faye's sake. "Listen, none of you have any proof Faye committed any kind of fraud. If you did, you'd have already called the police."

Owen scoffed. "You couldn't possibly know that."

"Am I wrong?"

After several tense moments, he slumped back in his seat. "No."

"Right." She rushed over and crouched beside Faye. "Are you okay?"

"I'm fine. Just embarrassed." She gestured toward the blond woman and her companion. "Getting dragged in front of the owners and not being able to help."

"Is Faye fired?" Alison asked the two strangers. Under other circumstances, she probably would've liked the woman. She had a sweet face and the dog seemed to adore her almost as much as the man at her side. Affection from an animal like that was usually well-deserved.

"No." The woman narrowed her blue gaze on Alison. "Not until we get to the bottom of this."

"Bottom found." Alison took Faye's hand and

straightened, pulling her friend to her feet. "She didn't do it. Neither did I. Come on, Faye. Let's go."

"Hey, wait a minute." Owen came around the desk, but they were already at the door. "Where are you going?"

Alison opened the door and shoved Faye out into the hallway then turned back to Owen. "Let me be clear. Anywhere you're not."

The tough guy's deep chuckle chased them both out into the hallway.

"Al, what's going on?"

Faye tried to stop, but Alison tugged her forward toward the casino floor. "Not here."

They walked out the front entrance and into the pandemonium that was the Fremont Street Experience. Once they'd taken a seat on a deserted bench, Alison turned to Faye. "Tell me exactly what happened."

"I don't know." Faye's pale complexion and shaking hands said otherwise. "They pulled me into the office and interrogated me about the whole cheating thing. I swear, Al, I don't know anything about it."

"I know." She took her friend's hand, hoping to calm her. "But why do they think you do?"

"Owen said my table gets an unusually high number of wins."

Because of me.

Guilt mingled with the tension already eating a whole in Alison's gut. "Did they threaten you at all?"

"No. Of course not." Faye took a deep breath and stared at the ground. "Owen's really nice, contrary to what you may think. So are Shelby and Chase. They just asked me a lot of questions and I guess I freaked out a little bit."

"Freaked out how?"

"They asked me about the players at the tables, if I noticed anything odd or had seen anything going on. I told them some of the players did win more often than others..." She winced. "That's when they said they had figures, video footage."

"Figures." She chuckled. "After talking to him last night, Owen Rockford wouldn't know how to interpret figures if his life depended on it. He goes with is gut, so from that aspect, you're fine."

Faye didn't look convinced. "I don't know. I mean, there's obviously someone cheating, right? Otherwise they wouldn't keep pursuing this."

For a brief second, Alison wished she could see those ledgers. If anyone could find the real culprit, it would be her. Chances of her getting her hands on Owen's data, or anything else after her little showdown in his office, however, were now slim to none. "C'mon." She stood and waited for Faye to do the same. "I need to check something."

It had been a few days since she'd last gotten a drop off, so another was due. She led Faye to the back of the casino building, through the parking lot and out to the bus hut. A quick search under the bench seat revealed another envelope taped in place, just like before. Alison tore it from its spot and opened it quickly, scanning the letter inside for clues.

"What's that?" Faye asked, holding a hand over her eyes. "I really need to get back inside. I've still got six hours left on my shift."

"Nothing." Alison tucked the letter inside her duffle then sighed, glad not to have found the code words that meant her cover had been blown. "It just means I have time to help you find this cheater."

"Oh." Faye followed Alison back toward the Lucky Ace. "What are you, some kind of a spy?"

Alison snorted. "Yeah, I'm a real super sleuth. Can't you tell? Too bad I'm not smooth or covert."

"Nope. Definitely not." Faye laughed and linked arms with her. "Did I mention I'm happy you're staying? For a little bit longer, at least."

"Thanks." They walked back into the cool interior of the casino again, the happy jingle of the slots at odds with Alison's solemn task ahead. "I need to convince your boss Owen to let me see those numbers he keeps talking about so I can find out who's the real cheater."

"Good luck with that." Faye pulled Alison over toward her assigned table. "What should I do?"

"Talk to the other dealers. See if they've noticed anything suspicious You guys see and hear everything, right?"

"Will do." Faye gave her a mock salute. "See you later?"

"Yep." Alison headed off to find a quiet place to concoct a new plan of attack. She needed to figure out a way to get a look at those numbers so she could clear Faye. She wouldn't be able to leave town until she knew the Rockfords no longer suspected that Faye had something to do with this cheater and it looked like the only way to do that was to find the person herself.

8

———

Back in his office, Owen continued to stare at the closed door. The girl had guts, he had to admit. No one waltzed into his office like that. No one.

"You really think she's the cheater?" Shelby asked, jarring him from his thoughts.

"Makes sense." He sat forward and folded his hands atop the desk. "She's friends with Faye and her number of wins at Faye's table are unusually high."

"I don't know." Shelby frowned. "Maybe she's just lucky. And Faye's been with us forever. I can't believe she'd do something like this."

"There's too much evidence to be pure coincidence."

"Still, it was brave of her to crash in here to rescue her friend. And Peaches went right over to Alison too. That says something about her integrity." Shelby scratched the dog behind the ears. "Doesn't it, girl?"

Chase placed a hand on Shelby's shoulder. "People get scared when they get caught and they do things they normally wouldn't, baby."

"No. She wasn't scared. Not about this, anyway." Shelby chuckled as Peaches rolled over at her feet, exposing her belly for a rub. "I'd say Ms. James is more of a cat person though. Perhaps a rag doll or a Siamese..."

Owen shook his head. "Lord save us from pet matchmakers."

Shelby looked up at him and grinned. "Never."

Peaches bounded to her feet and loped over to Owen next, all goofy dog grin and wagging tail. Unfortunately, he couldn't seem to resist her sweet canine charms and soon found himself petting her head while she rested her chin on his knee and gazed up and him with adoring eyes. He gave Shelby a critical look. "You're a nuisance, you know that?"

The dog whined and they all laughed.

"And so are you." His looked down at Peaches. After indulging in a few more doggy pats, he tried to steer the conversation back on track. "Look, this whole thing is too coincidental not to be true. Alison *always* plays at Faye's table. Why would she do that if not for the advantage?"

"They're friends," Shelby said, like it was the most obvious thing in the world.

"Yeah." Owen ordered Peaches back to her towel and toy in the corner then leaned back in his chair and clasped his hands atop his flat stomach. "And maybe she's taking advantage of that friendship."

"Jeez. What is it with you always thinking the worst of people?" Shelby's voice took on an uncharacteristic edge. "Seriously though, Owen. What real, concrete proof do you have that she's our cheater, other than your hunch? I learned to be a pretty good read of people from my dad, and nothing about her strikes me as thief material."

"Thief material? Do enlighten me." Owen crossed his arms, more to block out his own doubts about Alison being the cheater than anything else. "What exactly does that look like?"

Shelby mimicked his movements, clearly without an answer. "Smartass."

"Blake's the one who pointed all this stuff out and his opinion is good enough for me."

"Right," Chase chimed him, crossing his arms too. "Because Blake never has ulterior motives for bringing people together."

Owen scowled. "What the hell is *that* supposed to mean?"

"Think about it, man. Jan and Dino, Laura and Mike, me and Shelby." Chase placed his hand on her shoulder again and she took it, lacing their fingers together.

"Oh, God. Please tell me you're not implying my cousin did all of this to hook Alison and me up." He ignored the twinge of longing seeing Chase and Shelby so happy together created. He wasn't looking for another relationship. Not now. Maybe not ever. He'd been played one too many times. "Besides, Blake doesn't even know Alison. You're insane."

Chase gave a one-shoulder shrug. "Whatever you say, man."

"What I say is I'm not dating Alison or anyone else. Especially not while she's a suspect. End of story."

As if on cue, Peaches trotted over again and batted him on the leg with her paw.

"God, is everyone conspiring against me getting some actual work done today?" Owen reached down and scratched her behind the ears despite his harsh tone. "Can't you take her for me, Shelby?"

"Nope. I told you I fostered her out to Liv."

"How about finding her a better parent then, since my cousin doesn't seem all that interested in picking her up?"

Shelby leaned forward and grinned. "Are you volunteering?"

"Yeah, I am, actually." He grabbed the dog's leash off the corner of his desk and stood. "Volunteering to take her straight over to Liv's office. We'll see how she likes having her workday interrupted." Owen clipped the leash onto Peaches collar. "C'mon, girl. Let's take a walk to your mommy's office."

"Fine." Shelby sighed and sat back in her chair while Owen and Peaches walked toward the door. "But I'm sure if you change your mind, Liv would sign her over to you anytime. Peaches really likes you."

"Right. And I'm sure the fact you keep foisting her off on me has nothing to do with it." He opened the door and followed the dog out of the office. "Be back in a few."

Twenty minutes and numerous potty pit-stops later, Owen walked into the Rockford Security offices with Peaches by his side. The guards looked at the pair askance but didn't say a word. After all, they had to be too used to seeing Blake run around with a pet iguana on his shoulder to care.

He rode the elevator up to the executive suites with an antsy Peaches near his feet then made a beeline for Liv's office, barging in without knocking. "You lost your dog."

Olivia glanced up at him from over the top of a stack of paperwork and files, seemingly not at all surprised by his arrival. "I've got an idea. Why don't you shut the door and let her go? You call her. I call her. We'll see who she obeys."

Jaw tight, Owen clutched the leash tighter. "I don't have time for a pet right now. Not with my crazy work schedule."

"Shelby said you can bring her with you to the casino."

"And that sounds like a good idea to you?"

"No." Liv sat back, her smile sly. "It sounds like a fabulous idea to me. You need a woman in your life."

Dammit. Owen forced his tense shoulders to relax. "What I need are for people to mind their own damned business."

"Why?" Liv perked up. "Got a hot date I don't know about?"

"No." He shoved the images of Alison from his mind. "Don't be silly."

"Whatever. Nothing silly about love." Liv concentrated on her paperwork again. "Either take the dog or stop removing my decorations."

"How about you stop making my apartment into a frigging scrapbook? How about that?"

"How about you start acting like a part of this family again, Owen?" She tossed her pen down and glared at him. "We've stood by you through everything. All that mess with your discharge and then getting you the job at the Lucky Ace. Or have you forgotten all that already?"

They stared each other down from across the room, Peaches dancing nervous figure eights around his ankles from the palpable tension in the air.

"Hey, what's going on in here?" Blake poked his head through the open doorway, his voice hushed and his expression concerned. "Anything I can help with?"

"No." Owen knelt to tie Peaches leash around the leg of one of Liv's office chairs then straightened, stopping near Blake on his way out of the office. "Forget it. I was just leaving. Before somebody else tries to set me up on a date I don't want."

Blake looked from Owen to his sister, his tone droll. "Maybe you should take a look at your own life, sis, before you try your hand at matchmaking. You know, since you seem to have a lot of extra time to meddle in everyone else's." He stepped aside to avoid the crumpled up paper she hurled at his head. "Hey, you accuse me of doing the same thing all the time. I'm just sayin'."

Owen got the hell out of there before their sibling nosiness turned in his direction once more, but Liv called out to him on his way to the exit, halting his steps. "We love you, you know. So does Peaches. We only want what's best for you, Owen."

He turned back one last time after punching the elevator button. "I can take care of myself, thanks."

An hour later, Owen walked back into his office at the Lucky Ace. He'd stopped for lunch and even walked around the block a few times, all to clear his head and get back into the groove of a full work day.

Too bad none of it seemed to help.

He felt wrung out and fed up. So far, he'd looked into the background of any person on the casino's surveillance videos who even sneezed the wrong way and hadn't found diddly for proof of another cheater. Never mind Alison seemed a less likely candidate by the second. In all honestly, the only thing about her that still bothered him was that damned envelope he'd seen her take that night at the bus stop.

What the hell was in that thing? Money? Drugs? Worse?

Exhausted and frustrated, he stalked back toward his office only to be stopped by the guard on duty.

"Uh, sorry sir, but there's someone waiting for you," the guard said.

Owen gave him a dark stare. "There weren't any appointments on my calendar."

"Not a scheduled appointment, sir." The guard cocked his head toward Owen's door. "It's a suspect. Caught her lurking in near the security office. Should we call the police?"

He asked the question, though he feared he already knew the answer. "Did you get a name?"

"Her license said Alison James, sir."

Perfect. Stupendous.

Just what I need this afternoon. Another run-in with a prickly, pig-headed female.

He sighed loud and hard. "No police yet, Jeff. Thanks. I'll handle it."

"Yes, sir."

Owen opened the door to his office only to find Alison held between two guards, one on each arm. She looked pissed enough to do them serious bodily harm. He took in her flushed cheeks and glittering green eyes before shifting his attention to the guards. "That isn't necessary."

"But sir, we caught her snooping in the security office. We didn't want to risk her getting into your private things too."

"Let her go." Unfortunately, Alison James had gotten way more into his *private* things than he ever wanted or expected. She intrigued the hell out of him and infuriated him, all at the same time. Resigned to an afternoon of battle, he nodded. "It's fine. Thanks, guys. You can go. Ms. James and I have some things to discuss."

The guards left and Owen locked the door behind them, leaving him and Alison alone at last. He crossed his arms and leaned back against the wall. "So, you're a thief now as well as a cheater, huh?"

Alison's glare was cold enough to freeze mercury. "I wasn't stealing anything. I was trying to help you figure out the identity of your cheater."

"By sneaking into our private security office?"

"No. By watching the video footage."

She gave him an annoyed look, like he was some naughty kid or something. The idea of her admonishing him when she was clearly at fault pissed him off. Just when he'd started to think she might be honest after all.

"Listen," Alison continued. "I know a lot of players on the circuit—the ones who win and the ones who want to. But I can only see the action from my table. If I had access to the bird's eye view, I might be able to see a pattern. Who wins at what table, what they do after they win, all that. Then I could use math to calculate the probability of who might be your cheater."

Not the frigging math again.

Owen rubbed his eyes. "Remind me again why you want to help me?"

"Other than the fact you're trying to frame my best friend?"

"No one's trying to frame anyone. It's my job to discover the truth."

"Let me look at the surveillance footage." She stepped closer, her auburn curls bouncing. "Better yet, let me see the account ledgers."

"Sure. Right." Owen scrunched his nose at her request. "And maybe I'll let you into the vault too, help you pack up some more cash."

"Funny. Look, you've already admitted you hate math and I love it. I bet if you let me see the ledgers, I can tell you exactly who's swindling the casino."

He pushed away from the door and stalked past her to his desk. "What assurance do I have you won't point me in the wrong direction to keep yourself safe?"

She leaned her hands on one side of his desk and met his stare direct. "You'll just have to trust me."

"Trust you?" The words emerged harsher than he'd intended, but he was too tired to care. "Why should I trust you?"

"I'm not a cheater. I can show you that easily enough

with a deck of cards, and if you let me see the footage and ledgers, I'll prove that your cheater is someone else."

Owen narrowed his gaze. For whatever reason, this woman pushed all of his buttons without effort. Showing her private casino records would be risky enough. Still, her stalwart insistence that she was innocent piqued his interest. Most people caught with their hand in the cookie jar took the easy way out—pay the fine, lose their playing privileges.

She stared him down with steely resolve and he couldn't help but smile.

"Fine. I'll let you prove it. But not here. If I get caught showing you private internal accounting records, I'll be in even deeper shit with the owners. Meet me at my apartment at six tonight. I'll bring what you need." He jotted down the address and handed it to her. "Don't be late."

9

———

At six p.m. sharp, Alison knocked on Owen's apartment door. The building was nice enough, in a nice enough part of town too. Nothing fancy or ostentatious, the architecture fit him—clean, neat, to the point.

I like it. And him. More than I want to admit.

The door creaked open and Owen peeked out, still dressed in his suit from earlier, though he'd loosened his tie and unbuttoned the top two buttons of his shirt to expose a hint of the tanned flesh.

"Hey." He checked his watch. "Right on time."

"Of course." She waited until he opened the door then stepped inside his place. Glancing around, she was surprised. The interior of his apartment looked even less homey than her furnished rental. She'd expected him to be more of a family-type guy, but apparently she'd assumed wrong. From the mismatched furnishings to the moving boxes still unpacked against the walls, he seemed as ready to pick up and run as she did.

They walked over to an overstuffed sofa and each took a seat on opposite ends.

Owen pulled out a brand new deck of cards from his pocket, still in their crinkle wrap, and tossed them on the empty middle cushion. "Go ahead. Show me your magic."

"It's not magic. And it works better with two people." She opened the deck and handed the cards back to him. "You deal. Blackjack, five people at a table, just like at the Lucky Ace."

"Okay." He frowned, but did as she asked.

She scooted closer to see the cards better and their knees brushed. She shoved a slew of inconvenient feelings aside. For her and Faye's sake, she needed to focus on the numbers. She was here to find the real cheater before she left town. One last favor to a friend. Owen didn't factor into the equation. There was nothing long term here … or anywhere … for her. Ever.

Owen set the deck aside. "Now what?"

"I've got a near-photographic memory, meaning I can recall every card dealt in each progressive hand. And you already know I'm good at math and assessing probability. Right now, the only cards I don't know are what's in the dealer's hand, but that's where the probability comes in. Based on what's currently on the table, I'd say it's unlikely you're holding an ace." She pointed to the other four hands. "Because there's three already out. This is why I always try to sit last at whatever table I'm playing, or as close to last as I can. That way I can see what other cards come up and give myself a better chance to win." She glanced up at his slightly dazed expression. From the dark circles beneath his eyes and the shadow of stubble on his chiseled jaw, he looked pretty exhausted. *Poor baby.* Alison smiled and pointed at the deck. "Go ahead and deal the next round."

Once he did, she shook her head. "Look at all those faces. Now, I've only got eighteen, but from the cards showing and the calculations in my head, I'm guessing the dealer likely has less than that so I'm going to stay." She grinned. "Go ahead. Turn over the dealer's cards and see if I'm right."

Owen did and the hand showed a ten and two threes. Sixteen.

"Ha!" She clapped. "I win. No cheating involved."

He gathered up the cards, his gaze on her the whole time. "Counting cards *is* cheating."

"But I'm not counting cards. I'm guessing more than anything. Now maybe if there were more players, I'd have an edge, but the Lucky Ace keeps their player count at five per table, so no advantage here. Not to mention the fact your dealers shuffle between each hand, which makes it way harder to figure cards from past hands in my predictions. And if that still isn't enough proof, then how about each dealer changing to a fresh deck once an hour? Nope. Sorry. Your tables are practically bullet-proof, cheating-wise."

"Right." Owen relaxed back into the cushions, letting his head rest on the back of the sofa, his eyes half-lidded. "And yet, you're still able to win. Why is that?"

"Maybe I'm lucky."

"Maybe you're full of shit." He snorted. "Again?"

"Again."

They played at least six more hands over the next hour, each time with Alison explaining her strategy as she won. He seemed to grow more relaxed by the second and so did she. It was almost like sitting around with an old friend. Owen shuffled the cards.

"Again?" Owen's gaze drifted to her lips before returning to her eyes, and she got the distinct impression his thoughts weren't on cards.

She nodded, surprised to discover that she's somehow inched closer to him. "Again."

The word emerged husky.

Owned leaned closer, then hesitated. He pulled away, a shadow darkening his eyes. "What do you want from me?"

Her dazed brain struggled to comprehend his statement. The pure emotional part of her wanted to tell him to kiss her. The pure analytical side reminded her she was here to clear Faye's name. Reluctantly, she went with the truth. "I want to look at the numbers from the casino. I want to help you catch the real cheater."

Owen looked away. "Right. The numbers. That's why we're here. My bad."

"Yep." She briskly straightened her shirt ... along with her priorities. "That's why we're here."

He reached over the arm of the sofa and lifted up a briefcase. "I brought all the stuff I've been going over." He popped open the locks then pulled out a stack of ledger sheets. "The footage you'll have to look at on casino property, in my office. Downloading those would definitely send up red flags on my end, especially considering my cousin provides the feeds."

"Oh, yeah. Right." She tucked an errant curl behind her ear and did her best to focus on the sheets he'd handed her. He moved closer and peered over her shoulder, disturbing what little concentration she had left. "Listen, I can't do this while you're breathing down my neck."

Owen gave her a peeved look. "Why not? Can't think up a lie when I can point it out?"

"No. There is a little thing called personal space. You should look it up. Glorious concept, really. Could you get me something to drink though? My throat's dry."

He pushed to his feet. "What do you want?"

"Water's fine, thanks." Having a bit of space between them helped her frazzled nerves tremendously and while he tinkered in the kitchen, she studied the numbers. He returned a few minutes later, and took a seat beside her once more. She was about to ask him for some other useless thing when a scratching sounded started on the other side of his front door.

"Aw, hell no." He stalked over toward the entrance. "You have got to be kidding me."

"What is it?"

Owen opened the door and the dog from the casino scrabbled in, excited.

"The second most annoying female in this room."

"Nice." Alison reached over to pet the canine drooling on her feet "Hi, baby."

Owen took his seat once more and pulled out his cell phone, dialing with one hand while pushing the slobbering dog away from his face with the other. Whoever was on the other end of the line got an earful of angry. "Seriously? This is getting ridiculous. Even for you."

Scowling, he continued. "What? No. You know exactly what I'm talking about. Stop trying to set me up with a pet, okay? I don't need your help. I've got enough woman issues as it is."

Alison did her best to focus on the ledger sheets and not Owen's conversation, but her stubborn thoughts refused to obey.

He's got 'woman issues'? Is he seeing someone? Was that why he stopped kissing her?

Owen hung up and Alison pretended to work harder.

Awkward silence stretched between them until she

couldn't take it anymore. Finally, she addressed the huge elephant in their room, doing her best to keep her tone from betraying her inner curiosity. "Woman issues?"

"What?" He gave her some serious side-eye. "Forget it. It's none of your business."

"Fine." She tossed her hair over her shoulder and ran a finger down a column of figures. "If you didn't want to mess around on your girlfriend, you should've just said no."

"What?" He pressed the heels of his hands into his eyes and leaned back into the sofa cushions. "Which part of 'none of your business' didn't you understand?"

"Whatever."

"Stop prying into my life and just do what you came her to do, okay?"

"I already have."

"Huh?" He straightened, looking far more alert now. "Already? How?"

She grabbed a nearby highlighter. "Look at these transactions. They're done on different days at different times. They seem random, but there's a pattern. The sums start out modest, but increase exponentially as the months go by. Now, they're running in the high five to low six figure range."

"Great." He squinted at the columns she'd pointed out. "Still doesn't tell me who the culprit is, though."

"Run these amounts against the cashier tapes from the same dates. That'll nab your cheater." She gave him a satisfied smile. "These guys think they're smart, that they're being random enough not to get caught, but with enough data—and time—a pattern emerges. Only computers are truly random. People are biased."

"Shit." Owen walked over to a laptop on his kitchen table. He punched the keys on the keyboard then whistled. "Goddamn. I don't think it's just one person."

"No?" She joined him, but he shooed her away before she could see anything more than the fact he was logged into the casino's intranet system. "Why?"

"Because there are two different players club accounts listed with these transactions."

"Interesting." She slumped against the wall and pretended to study her nails while taking another quick glance at the screen. One name jumped out at her. Greg Walpole. "You think they're working together?"

"Could be. And I might know who one of them is too, but I need more proof."

"I gave you all the proof right there." She pointed at the ledger sheets still covering the sofa cushions, irritated. "What more do you want?"

"You gave me the transactions." He closed the laptop and faced her, one muscular forearm resting on the back of his chair. "I still need to tie them to the right people and prove they're suspicious."

"Fine. I'll let you get to it then." She walked back over to the sofa and grabbed her purse.

"Thanks for this. I'll call Blake and get his team on it right away. We'll find the real guilty parties."

"And clear Faye's name?"

And mine.

"Yep. If you guys are innocent, you've got nothing to worry about."

He'd already reopened the laptop and was typing away as she let herself out.

***

THE NEXT AFTERNOON, Alison burst into Faye's apartment with her laptop under her arm. It was easy enough to dig into someone's past—if you had the time, their name, and a steady internet connect. Right now, she had the first two, but not the third. Thankfully, that's where her best friend came in handy. She plopped down on one end of Faye's couch and fired up her computer again without so much as saying hello.

Faye, still in her PJs at nearly two in the afternoon, gave Alison a disbelieving look. "Um, what the hell are you doing?"

She remained focused on her task, clearing both of their names of any wrongdoing. "Cyberstalking someone."

"Right." Faye took a sip of her coffee, watching Alison over the rim. "And you feel the need to do that in my apartment why?"

"Ms. Baker doesn't have the greatest Internet. Keeps cutting out all the time. And this isn't exactly stuff I want to do in front of an entire café full of people." She typed in new searches at lightning speed, speaking to Faye over her shoulder without really looking at her. "Did you find out anything from the other dealers?"

"Yeah, I did, as a matter of fact."

She paused in her typing, finally glancing at Faye with a raised brow. "And?"

"And you know that creep who hit on you the other day? The one who wouldn't let you leave? I found out he wins a lot, at all the tables. One of the gals said he's there sometimes with another guy—blond, medium build. Not sure if you've seen them together at a table or not."

"Huh." After leaving Owen's, she'd run the name she'd seen on his screen—Greg Walpole—and managed to match his face to the creep Faye mentioned. The partner thing, though, was new. Alison frowned and went back to typing. If Walpole was working with a partner, that would make sense. Two takes were better than one. And less suspicious.

"Want me to make some lunch?" Faye headed for the kitchen. "I need to eat before my shift at five."

"Yeah, sure." She kept her attention on her screen, scrolling through new data. "I could eat."

"Omelet or salads?"

"Whatever."

"Cool."

Amidst the sounds of cookware clacking and food sizzling, Alison dug deeper into Greg Walpole. She started with social media—Facebook, Twitter, Instagram. You could live off the grid. Hell, she was proof of that. But most people liked to stay in touch. But after several minutes of looking, she remained empty-handed.

Faye returned and set a plate of veggie omelet and toast on the coffee table in front of Alison then took the seat beside her. "How's it going?"

"Slow."

"You should take a break. Eat your food before it gets cold."

Alison wanted to keep working, but her rumbling stomach said otherwise. Reluctantly, she set the laptop aside and picked up her plate and fork. "Hey, I didn't know you were into adultery."

"What?" Faye halted mid-chew. "What are you talking about?"

"Your Rockford McHottie." Alison dug into the creamy eggs and crunchy veggies, savoring the salt and greasy goodness and the spicy snap of the peppers. "He's got a girlfriend."

"Owen? You must be kidding." Faye spoke around a bite of toast, her words muffled. "He spends more time at the casino than I do. No way does *that* guy have a social life."

"All I know is, he turned me down pretty quick." She

took a sip of the orange juice Faye had brought out with her food.

Faye's brow rose. "You mean that night in the bar? I didn't realize anything happened when I was up by the stage. You were drunk, though. Maybe he was trying to be a gentleman."

"Was not," Alison mumbled under her breath, cursing herself for bringing up her second rendezvous with Owen the day before.

Idiot.

Mortified, heat prickled Alison's cheeks and she looked away fast.

"Like hell you weren't." Faye chuckled and licked her fork then stared at Alison. "Wait a minute. You saw him again, didn't you? I can tell from your face. When?"

"Yesterday. I didn't do it very well though, apparently."

"You like him!" Faye laughed. "I knew there was something between you two."

"There's nothing between us, okay?" Alison stuffed her last bite of eggs in her mouth, then wiped her face with a napkin and set the plate back on the table. "He's hot, that's all. And it's been a while..." She sat back and crossed her arms, feeling way more vulnerable than she liked. Embarrassed, Alison picked up her laptop again and continued searching for more dirt on Walpole.

Faye laughed. "You and Owen are perfect for each other. Man, am I a matchmaker or what?"

"At this point, I'd go with 'or what'." She ignored her friend's obscene gesture and continued typing. "Owen Rockford and I are not perfect. You are not a matchmaker. It was a fleeting moment and nothing really happened."

"Uh-huh."

Ignoring her, Alison continued to type. "Dammit." Alison scowled at her computer screen, exasperated. "I hate Facebook. Faye, what's your login? It won't let me see anything unless I'm signed in."

"You don't have Facebook?"

The aghast tone of her friend's voice broke through Alison's grumpy fog and she laughed. "Don't act so surprised. It is possible to live without it, you know."

Especially with Copernatech looking for me.

"Here." Faye held out her hand and Alison handed over the laptop, watching while her friend typed in her credentials then she gave the computer back.

It was a long shot, given the guy's penchant for cheating, but the results popped up and there was a Greg Walpole's profile listed in Vegas. Perhaps her crap luck was turning around. Once his page loaded, Alison scoured his friend list for blond men.

"So." Faye got up to take their dishes to the kitchen. "How are you going to snag Owen?"

"What?" She scrolled through picture after picture with no luck. Boy, for a guy who liked to live on the down low, Walpole sure as hell had a lot of online friends. "I'm not trying to snag anyone. Particularly not a guy with a girlfriend."

"Like I said." Faye returned to her seat. "I'd bet good money he's just playing hard to get."

Only half-paying attention to her friend, Alison stopped near the bottom of Greg's friend list, hovering over a picture of a blond guy who looked vaguely familiar. *Cory Springer*. She clicked on his name and saw him listed as Greg's half-brother. She turned the screen to face Faye. "Is this the other guy, the one the dealer saw?"

Faye leaned in and squinted. "Yeah, looks like him."

Grinning, Alison sat back and closed the laptop. "Bingo! We just found the real cheaters."

10

The next day, Owen leaned against the wall in his office, watching while the casino's top IT guy clacked away on his computer keyboard. The guy looked about twelve and was dressed the same way, but given the information Alison had discovered, he'd decided it was best to follow her trail. Her theory of Walpole having a partner made sense too, even if he still wasn't one-hundred-percent convinced Alison might not be the partner in question.

The office door opened and Shelby and Chase walked in, glancing from the IT guy to Owen, then back again.

"Who's he?" Shelby asked.

"Ronny's my best tech guy. He's been here over an hour and we think there are two cheaters. He's searching the video surveillance and databases for anyone associated with the one known suspect, Greg Walpole. If he's got a partner, Ronny should be able to discover their identity."

"You have a name now too?"

"Yep." Owen pulled out the ledger sheets Alison had highlighted. "See these transactions? We've pinpointed at least half of them to a player's club account under the name of Gregory Walpole. The other half use a different number, but they're all the same. So, if we can connect the dots, we should be able to bust them both."

"Wow." Shelby gave him an impressed smile. "Good work, Owen."

"Thanks." Much as he wanted to take all the credit, his honor wouldn't let him. "I had help though. From Alison."

"The cute math whiz who came to her friend's rescue?" Chase asked, winking at Shelby. "Maybe Blake was right."

Owen shook his head, disgruntled. "No. Blake was not right. There is nothing between Alison and me, except the fact she's good at math."

"So." Shelby took a seat in one of the chairs in front of his desk. "We need to figure out who the other guy is and get a name, right? Seems pretty straightforward."

"Yeah." Owen scrubbed a hand over his face. "Except even if we find these guys, we still have to prove that they're cheating."

"Daddy was always big on everyone enrolling in the

player's club when they came into the casino. Said it made things easier to track for us and gave them big incentives to spend more cash in the place. We give them double points for showing the card when they collect their winnings. Numbers don't lie." She turned to Ronny, who remained completely focused on the screen before him. "Can you get into that database, Ronny?"

"Nope. Sorry. Not without the security code, ma'am."

"Good thing I'm here then." She grabbed a sticky pad and pen off Owen's desk and scribbled down six digits then slid them over to the IT guy. "There you go."

"Awesome. Just a sec and I'll be in…" He typed furiously then sat back, frowning. "Hmm…"

"Hmm what?" Owen peered over his shoulder. "Find something?"

"Can I see those ledger sheets again, Mr. Rockford?" Ronny asked.

"Sure." He handed them to the kid then leaned back while his tech guru typed some more. Owen liked surfing the Net as much as the next guy, but this kid was a computer geek extraordinaire.

"Yes!" Ronny grinned wide and pointed at the screen. "Found 'em. They used their club card here, here, and here."

"Great." Chase came around the desk to stand beside Owen. "Can we get a visual on them from the cameras?"

"Maybe." Owen squinted at the screen. "What's the name, Ronny? If we can track their movements through the card, we can pinpoint which camera locations to check."

"Um." Ronny hit a few more keys then sat back. "Looks like an A. James."

"What?" His blood froze in his veins. "Say that again?"

"A. James."

Cursing, Owen slumped against the wall. "We don't need a visual. I know who that is."

"Who?" Shelby leaned closer, her expression concerned.

"Alison."

"Oh.. right. A for Alison." Shelby's face creased. "Are you sure? She doesn't seem like a cheater."

"Damn." Chase leaned in closer over Ronny's shoulder. "Yep. She cashed in those chips. No doubt about it. What do you want us to do?"

Anger and hurt stabbed Owen's chest and he reacted from pure instinct and betrayal. "Get her photo to security. If she's dumb enough to come in here again, we'll have her arrested."

"Stop here, driver."

Alison paid the cab fare then climbed out near the bus stop behind the Lucky Ace. Another envelope was due from her contact today, so she peered under the bench once the taxi had gone.

Nothing yet, but it was still early.

Determined to tell Owen her good news, she rushed across the parking lot toward the back entrance to the casino.

Finally, she could walk into this place without feeling like a dead man walking.

She couldn't wait to see if they'd caught the bad guys. Visiting the casino had nothing to do with the spark she'd felt between her and Owen, she just wanted to hear him say that she and Faye were innocent.

Practically floating on an air of confidence, she stepped inside the shadowed casino and headed for the hallway where Owen's office was located.

Too bad there could never be anything between her and Owen Rockford. When the smoke cleared, she would still be on the run from Copernatech. Her fuzzy interlude in Vegas couldn't last forever.

11

———

"Wait a minute." Shelby pushed to her feet and joined Chase behind the computer. "You can't arrest her based just on this. What happened to proving she's a cheater first?"

Oh, she's a cheater all right. Just like Faith...

Still, much as Owen hated to admit it, Shelby was right. "Fine. I'll go down to the cashier window and talk to the employee who handled the transactions. That'll give us both video surveillance and an eye witness putting Alison on the scene. Coupled with the ledger transactions she pointed out herself, and we should have enough to get the cops to haul her in for questioning."

"I don't know." Shelby shook her head and crossed her arms. "I'm still not convinced. Why would she call attention to the ledger transactions if it would implicate her."

"Arrogance." Owen pushed to his feet and paced the room a seed of doubt creeping in. Alison wasn't arrogant, so why would she point out that entry? But there was mounting evidence against her. "There was video of Alison at Faye's table. Walpole was there too. She sat close to him and now I know why. We've confirmed he's the other culprit, so it makes sense."

"Um, Mr. Rockford?"

"What?" Owen did his best to hide his growing agitation and failed miserably, if the way the kid flinched was any indication. "Sorry. What is it, Ronny?"

"Someone just made another big transaction with this club card."

"Really?" Owen stepped in on the kid's other side to stare at the computer screen. "When? What cashier?"

"A few minutes ago," Ronny said. "Around three forty-five. Let me check the security camera near there."

While he watched Ronny zip through several pages of video feeds, Owen was torn between excitement and despair. Excitement over finally catching a break on the cheaters, and despair that all fingers pointed to Alison. Before he could wallow in his feelings, however, the phone on his desk rang. "Yes?"

"Sir, we're tracking your suspected cheater on the casino floor now. Should we apprehend her?"

Alison. Eyes squeezed shut and muscles tight with tension, Owen nodded. "Yes. Pick her up. Do not let her get away." He slammed the phone down and turned to the others. "She's here. Ronny, get that video from the cashier's cage as soon as possible. I'm going to head out there and—"

The office door burst open. One of the security guards held up a manila envelope similar to the one Owen had seen Alison nab that night behind the casino. "Sorry, sir, but Blake Rockford said you needed this information right away."

He snatched the envelope from the guy and tore it open then scanned the contents fast. "When did you find this?"

"About three forty, sir. Five minutes before the redhead showed up to retrieve it."

"Wait!" Shelby shouted. "If Alison was outside getting this envelope at three forty-five, there's no way she could've cashed in those chips."

"She's right, sir." Ronny swiveled the monitor to face Owen. "The video shows a blond guy using that card just now, not a woman."

"Goddammit!" Owen bolted from the room, praying he had time to find Alison before his security guards.

✦ ✦ ✦

ELBOWING her way through yet another crowd of players, Alison headed toward the back of the casino and Owen's office. The place was crazy busy this afternoon for some reason. Crowds were definitely not her forte, mainly because it made it that much harder to spot any Copernatech bad guys lurking about.

She weaved through a raucous bunch of senior citizens having a heyday at the penny slots and stepped out into a small open spot. Taking a deep breath at last, she glanced around only to find two black suited security guards watching her from a nearby alcove. One of them whispered toward the earpiece on his right side then both started toward her.

Her blood froze. What could they want with her?

Not wanting to wait around to find out, she panicked and turned to flee and smashed right into a six-foot wall of pure, hard muscle. She looked up and met a pair of familiar brown eyes.

Owen.

He waved off the guards and took her arm, guiding her toward the opposite wall where it was quieter. She tried to pull free but his grip was too firm. "What's going on?"

"We found the cheaters."

"Me too. That's why I'm here. I wanted to tell you so you could—" A blond guy raced behind Owen and her eyes widened. "Oh, my God! That's him! Cory Springer, Walpole's partner. You need to stop him before he gets away!"

"Stay here," Owen warned before rushing after the guy.

Not wanting to risk her one shot at clearing her and

Faye's names, Alison followed right behind Owen. If Cory Springer tried something, she'd happily bust out all of her self-defense karate skills on his sorry ass. Might help her work out some aggression too.

Owen raced for the front entrance while she took a detour toward the side door. Walpole and Springer were smart. Far too smart to run out right beneath security's noses. The side exit seemed a much likely probability.

Sure enough, she made it to the door at the same time as Springer and managed to catch him by surprise. He went for a classic around-the-waist hold on her, thinking she was some small, helpless female.

Big mistake.

He no sooner had his arms around her then she went for the SING—solar plexus, instep, nose, groin—then finished with a nice roundhouse kick that sent him flying through the glass door. She reached out to catch him by the scruff of his shirt collar but ended up cutting her arm on the shards still hanging on the door frame instead.

"Ow! Shit." She hissed and scowled down at Springer's now unconscious form lying in a sea of glass on the pavement. After a kick to his shin for good measure, she turned to find a stunned Owen and his crew watching her, along with Shelby, Chase, Blake and another woman who shared the Rockford family's coloring and good looks, but whom she'd never met. "What?"

"Damn," the unknown woman said. "We missed it."

"Not now, Liv." Blake stepped forward and wrapped his handkerchief around Alison's now oozing cut. "We heard something was going down at the Lucky Ace and rushed over to help. Thanks to you, it looks like it's all taken care of."

She replaced his hand with hers on her injured forearm and applied pressure as best she could. The damned thing was really starting to hurt. "Thanks. I got it."

"Yeah." Chase stepped forward to look Springer over. "Thanks to Alison's help here, we figured out who the cheaters are and caught them."

"Yes. Thanks so much, Alison." Shelby moved in beside her. "Oh, gosh. Your arm looks pretty bad. Let me call the house doctor over to take a look at it."

"No, no. I'm fine." She inched away. "Really. It's nothing."

Chase took her hand and lifted it away along with the now soaked handkerchief. "No. That's a nasty cut. You need to go to the ER. Probably needs stitches."

As much as she hated crowds, hospitals were even worse. Hospitals kept records and medical records could lead Copernatech right to her doorstep. "Honestly, I'm fine. I'll just bandage it up and I'm all good."

The woman Blake had called Liv piped up next. "You know, I installed a brand new first aid kit at Owen's apartment. Fully stocked and raring to go. His place is right around the corner too."

Blake took her elbow gently and guided Alison toward the front door before she could protest. "Sounds like a plan." It wasn't until she was standing outside the casino that Alison realized he'd hauled Owen out too right alongside her. He gave them both a slight push on the back before heading back inside. "You guys go take care of her arm. I'll handle things here."

"What about the police reports and the paperwork and—"

"I got it," Blake said, holding up a hand to severe Owen's excuses. "Ex-police force, remember? Besides, there's nothing here you can't handle later, cuz. Go take care of what's important."

"He's right." Shelby joined them outside. "In fact, take the rest of the day off. You've been working non-stop the past couple of weeks and deserve a break after this. I'll handle any questions for now."

"Go on." Blake waved them off. "Go. We'll take care of it and I'll call you if anything comes up, okay? Owen, take care of Alison. You owe her, especially after she did you a big favor by stopping that guy. Show her some appreciation."

Alison

was too tired to argue now that her adrenaline buzz was wearing off. Plus, her arm stung like a son of a bitch. Dazed and slightly shaky, she allowed Owen to lead her through the covered Fremont Street Experience and out into the bright sunshine beyond.

12

———

"So, uh, here we are again." Owen unlocked the door to his apartment and gestured for Alison to enter ahead of him. "I wasn't expecting company, so, forgive me if it's kind of a mess."

He closed the door behind him and shook his head, glad she couldn't see his face. Jesus, he was babbling like some teenaged kid, all because he'd brought a pretty girl home. Sighing, he dropped his keys on a side table and shoved his hands in his pockets.

Correction.

Not pretty. Gorgeous.

Even with one arm all trussed up like a Thanksgiving turkey and her hair wild from the altercation at the casino, she looked like his every fantasy come to life. Owen cleared his throat to loosen the sudden constriction and forced a weak smile. "Can I get you something to drink?"

Alison stood in the middle of his living room, staring at the wall of family pictures Liv had put up. "No. I'm good, thanks. I would like to get this cleaned up though." She raised her injured forearm. "Can you show me where that first aid kit is?"

"Right, sure." He led her back to the bathroom where he'd stowed the kit under the sink. Hoping to make amends for suspecting her of being the cheater, he pointed toward the ledge of his bathtub. "Have a seat. That's kind of an awkward spot to do things yourself. I'll help."

She did as he asked, if somewhat reluctantly. While he fished out the first aid kit, along with several clean towels and a washcloth, he tried to keep the banter light. "So, where'd you learn to fight? Those were some pretty impressive skills you showed back there."

"Oh." Alison frowned and looked away. "Self-defense classes."

"Rough neighborhood where you're from?"

"Something like that."

Her non-answer made him swivel slightly to glance at her. Dots of pink now flushed her cheeks and dark smudges colored the delicate skin beneath her eyes. She looked as stressed and exhausted as he was.

An unexpected wave of protectiveness surged through him and he gathered the things to patch her arm then knelt in front of her. Gingerly, Owen grasped her forearm and started to peel back the bloody handkerchief tied around it.

"Ouch!" She clenched her teeth, her gaze lowered, and her brows drawn together. "It really stings."

"I'm sorry." Once the cloth was gone, the cut started to bleed again, but thankfully after he got it cleaned up it wasn't as deep as he'd originally thought. He'd seen his share of wounds in combat and this one didn't look like it would need stitches. "This might hurt a bit, but we need to make sure it's clean so it doesn't get infected."

Owen dabbed a cotton pad soaked in antibacterial solution around the area, doing his best to concentrate on keeping his touch gentle and light and not think about how silky her skin felt beneath his fingertips.

Nose wrinkled, Alison squeezed her eyes shut and looked away. "Thanks for helping me. It would've been hard to do it myself. You were right."

"Say that again."

"What?"

"The last part." He glanced up at her and grinned. "It's not something a man hears too often. I just want to savor the moment."

At last, her serious expression cracked into a wide smile as he tossed the soiled cotton pads into the trash and opened several packages of sterile gauze to cover the cut. "Funny. Where'd you learn to play nursemaid?"

"Military." His answer came out more clipped than

he'd wanted, but his past wasn't something he wanted to discuss. "We all got trained in basic first aid and wound care."

"What branch?"

"Marines." He straightened and picked up the supplies. "Ok. That should be good to go."

"Right." She nodded and stared at the floor. From her confused, slightly hurt expression she'd taken his abruptness as a rejection. He felt bad about that until he remembered how much beautiful women could hurt you. *Better to leave this one alone.*

"Um, thanks." She started to get up then swayed slightly on her feet.

Owen spotted her near collapse in the mirror and caught her before she hit the floor. "Hey. You okay?"

"Sorry," she mumbled. "I'm feeling dizzy all the sudden."

She tried to push him away, but he held fast. No way was he letting her hurt herself even more on his behalf today. Slipping one arm around her back and the other under her knees, he picked up her slight weight and carried her out into the living room then placed her on the sofa where they'd sat the day before.

"You rest a minute, okay?" He took her hands in his, frowning at their cold, clammy feel. Maybe she'd done more than cut her arm on the glass.

He covered her with an afghan from the back of the

sofa then stepped back. "I'll, uh, finish in there then be right back."

"Okay."

Her voice sounded weak and quiet, so different from the spitfire he was used to. His worry skyrocketed. "You'll be all right while I'm gone?"

She nodded and he rushed back to the bathroom to clean up the rest of their mess in record time. When he returned, thankfully, her color had returned and she seemed more alert. He took off his suit jacket and tie, loosening the top buttons on his shirt and his cuffs.

"Want something to drink now? How about food? When's the last time you ate?" Owen rolled up his shirt-sleeves and headed into his open kitchen. "I haven't had time to hit the grocery store recently but I think I can throw together something."

"I had an omelet earlier at Faye's."

"Okay." He peered in his fridge and spotted some leftover nachos from his dinner the night before. "Um, how about Mexican? You like nachos?"

"Love 'em." Alison tried to sit up then fell back against the cushions. "But don't go to any trouble."

"No trouble at all." Owen removed the carryout container from the fridge then gave her his best mock stern look. "And you stay there, missy. That's an order."

"Yes, sir."

"Good girl."

While he set about heating up their dinner, he heard

her click on the TV. Soon the sounds of the nightly news reports filled the air.

"Hey, the Lucky Ace bust is on the nightly news."

"Yeah?"

Good. Dirty cheaters.

If he had his way, he'd plaster the pictures of Walpole and his accomplice up all over town so that bastard would never be able to play in Vegas again. He split the sizable portion of nachos into equal halves on two separate plates, added a dollop of salsa to each, then carried their food into the living room. "Here you go."

"Yum! Thanks so much." Alison sat up, steadier this time and gobbled up a chip full of stringy cheddar cheese. "Mmm. These are so good."

Owen went back to the kitchen to grab their beverages and some napkins. "What do you want to drink?"

"Whatever you're having is fine."

"Pale ale?"

"Perfect."

He returned with two chilled bottles and a stack of napkins then took a seat a safe distance away on the opposite end of the sofa. As he dug into his food, he realized he really was starving. With the craziness of the day, he'd not had a chance to eat at all. Unfortunately, it wasn't an uncommon occurrence. Good for the waistline, not so good for life in general. Mouth full, he hazarded a glance at Alison and found her stuffing her face as well.

He always did love a woman with a healthy appetite.

He was so busy watching her, that he wasn't watching his own food. The chip in his hand tilted, spilling cheese and beans and salsa all down the front of his clean white shirt. "Shit."

"Oh." Alison set her plate aside and squinted at the stain. "Have any seltzer water?"

"I think there's some in the fridge. Why?"

"My turn to help." She set her now empty plate on the coffee table in front of them then got up and went into the kitchen, coming back with a bottle of water and a dishtowel. She brushed his hands away from where he was only making the mess worse and poured water on the towel before dabbing it against the greasy stain on his chest. "Seltzer water helps keep it from setting."

"Huh." The word squeaked out past his rigid vocal cords. Frazzled, he grabbed her hand and took the towel. "I can get it now. Thanks."

"Oh, sure." She sat back, bringing her lips within inches of his. "Whatever you want."

What he wanted was to pull her closer and kiss her senseless, but that seemed about as wise as jumping off a hundred story building.

"Sorry." She moved back to her corner of the sofa and clutched the afghan tight around her. "I didn't mean to..." Alison tossed her long red curls over her shoulder and stared straight ahead at the TV screen. "You know. I mean, with your girlfriend and all."

"Girlfriend?" He leaned forward to set the water and

towel on the table beside his plate. "What the hell are you talking about?"

"The woman today, the pretty brunette. What was her name? Liv?"

"Okay, ewww. Liv's my cousin." Owen stood and untucked his shirt to help it dry, then sat back down and toed off his shoes before stretching out his legs. He clasped his hands atop his full stomach and stared at the TV without really seeing it. His full attention, for better or worse, was zeroed on the woman a mere five feet away.

"Hmm." Alison shifted in her seat and one of her feet brushed the side of his thigh. Without thinking, he reached out and grabbed it, massaging it gently. "Oh. That feels amazing."

Neither of them spoke for a while. Her, eyes closed and head back against the sofa cushions, him soothing her tense muscles.

At last, she peeked one eye open and peered over at him. "Woman issues."

"What?" He moved his hand from her foot to her ankle, still kneading her tense muscles.

"You mentioned woman issues the other day…" The dreamy, breathless quality of her voice only added to his haze.

"I've dated my share of women in the past."

"I'm sure you have."

"What's that supposed to mean?"

She coughed and tried to pull away, but he wouldn't let her. Not yet. He slid his fingertips higher to rub circles on her calf. This time her words rushed out in a slightly nervous tumble. "Nothing. I just, well, I just meant that a good-looking guy like you, well, you probably have tons of women lined up to be with you. That's all."

Owen smiled, working her tired muscles with gentle pressure. Good to know he wasn't the only one affected by their interactions. "You think I'm good looking?"

"Maybe a little." She teased then gasped as his fingers moved to her knee, but he shushed her like a skittish colt.

"Easy." He scooted closer for better reach. "Does that feel good?"

"Yes."

"Good." Owen leaned closer still, bringing his mouth millimeters from hers, then said her name, his voice reverent like a prayer. "Alison."

"I should go," she said, shattering his hazy happiness.

"What? No. Why?" He tightened his hand on her knee. "Stay. I thought we were having a good time."

"We are, but..."

"If I'm taking it too far..." He stroked the silky skin of the inside of her knee.

"You didn't." Her words were so soft he almost didn't catch them. She bit into her lower lip. "It's just ... I'm afraid if I stay, then I won't want to leave."

There was still a lot of unfinished business between

them. Things she didn't know about him. Things he didn't know about her. But at that moment, none of it carried weight. Owen stared into the brilliant green eyes that had so captured him from the start and said the only two words that mattered. "Then don't."

ALISON BLINKED into the bright sunshine, then squinted around the unfamiliar room. Her heart raced as panic set in.

Where am I? What happened? Did Copernatech find me?

It took a moment for her drowsy brain to catch up with her pounding pulse, but when it did she flopped back onto the mattress and groaned.

Owen's. I'm at Owen's.

He'd helped her bandage her arm, fed her dinner, and then... Smiling, she stretched beneath the covers then stared at the white ceiling above. Well, she was certainly thinking clearly again. And that meant...

Yeah, time to go.

Definitely.

With the sheet wrapped around her, she got out of bed and scrounged for her clothes. After slipping them on, she went in search of her shoes. If memory served, they were in the living room. All she had to do was sneak out there and slip them on and she could get out of here before Owen discovered she was gone.

Speaking of gone, where was he?

His side of the bed had been cold when she'd checked, meaning he'd gotten up long before she'd awakened.

Work maybe?

She padded out to the living room and stopped short.

"Mornin'." He winked at her from the open kitchen. "Sleep good?"

So much for sneaking out unnoticed. And didn't he just look fine all tousled and stubbly wearing a plain white tee-shirt and a kiss-the-cook apron. She took a seat to put on her sneakers. Her arm still stung from the cut, but nothing nearly as bad as the day before. "Yep. Slept fine, thanks. And you?"

"Like a baby."

She smoothed her hands through her hair then tucked them beneath her, unsure how to act or what to say in this situation.

"Hope you like eggs and bacon."

"Sure." Her stomach growled despite her awkwardness. "Can I help with anything?"

"You can set the table if you want.'

"Okay." She walked into the kitchen and grabbed plates and silverware and napkins from the places he pointed, then did as he'd asked. "What about drinks?"

"I've got my coffee already." He held up his mug. "But help yourself to whatever you'd like."

"Coffee's good for me too." She fixed herself a mug—

black, nothing added—then leaned against the edge of the counter while he served up their food. "What time do you have to go to work today?"

"It's Friday, so a late shift for me. I don't go in until around noon. How about you? Got big plans for the weekend?"

"No." She sipped her mug then took her plate and followed him to the table. "Just the usual."

"What's the usual?"

"Just stuff. Nothing interesting."

They each dug into their food, keeping the conversation light and impersonal.

After he'd finished his last bite of toast, he narrowed his gaze. "We should go to dinner tonight. You know, so I can repay you for helping me catch Walpole."

"Dinner?" She swallowed hard to avoid choking on her eggs. Spending the night was one thing, moving beyond that to...*more*, was something else entirely. "Um, okay. Sure. Dinner's good. Tonight's out though."

"Got another hot date?" He watched her closely. "We didn't really discuss your end of things."

"No, no date." She didn't want to lie to him, but she couldn't tell him the truth either. *"There's a bunch of crazed, homicidal pharmacy execs who want me dead,"* wasn't exactly first-date fodder. "I have some errands I need to take care of. Rain check?"

"Okay, sure. No problem." He stood and cleared their plates.

She could tell from his now shuttered expression that he'd taken her refusal as more than a no, but there wasn't much she could do given the current circumstances. With the precarious nature of her life at present, cooling things off between them was probably for the best anyway, no matter how much it hurt to let him go and move on.

"Well." Alison pushed to her feet and grabbed her hoodie from the back of his sofa where she'd thrown it yesterday afternoon. The sleeve was ripped where the glass had sliced through it and she'd have to patch it when she got back to her apartment, but still, the garment gave her a modicum of comfort and protection against the harsh world outside. "I should, um, probably go and get out of your hair."

"Sure." He walked toward her and her heart kicked into overdrive.

He's going to kiss me. God, yes, please let him kiss me just once more.

Except he didn't.

Instead, Owen brushed past her and opened the front door. "See you later, then."

"Yeah." She walked out into the hall and turned to say goodbye, but he'd already shut the door. She leaned her back against the opposite wall and whispered, "See ya."

The ride in the elevator down to the lobby of his

building passed in a blur. Lost in her thoughts, she headed outside and into the bright Vegas morning.

Faye.

She needed to talk to her best friend, work out what had happened the night before, figure out where to go from here. Faye's apartment was only a few blocks away and the day was warm. No reason she couldn't make the short walk.

No reason except the nagging tingle on the back of her neck.

Someone's watching me again.

Scanning the crowd around her, Alison didn't spot anyone in particular, but that didn't mean Copernatech hadn't caught up with her at last.

Nervous, she hailed a cab for the short ride to her apartment instead. If they had found her, if her time in Vegas was up, she needed to leave without a trace, which ruled out going to Faye's.

Once the taxi pulled up near the curb at Ms. Baker's, she paid the fare, then let herself in to her basement abode. Hell, she hadn't even had time to unpack from her last almost-bail. The only difference this time would be when she left town, no one would ever find her again.

13

—————

"Hey!" Faye said, her smile quickly dissolving into a frown. "What's wrong?"

Alison pushed inside, her heavy duffle bag in tow. She'd tossed and turned all night. Her mind on Owen's cold reaction when she'd told him she'd have to take a raincheck for dinner. Maybe he'd sensed she would never come through on that. What did it matter? She'd never see him again because she had to leave town. She'd seriously considered just going without seeing Faye too, but deep friendship and the fact she'd left her computer here had stopped her. "Nothing. I need my laptop."

"What's with the bag then?" Faye closed the door then leaned back against it, arms crossed. "And the hunted attitude. I know you, girlfriend. Something's wrong."

"No, you don't," Alison mumbled, tossing throw pillows aside on the sofa in search of her missing computer. Locating it stuck between two seat cushions, she pulled it out and unzipped the side pocket on her duffle to shove it inside. "You don't *know* me. Not really. No one does."

"You're leaving again, aren't you?" Faye raised a speculative brow, not budging from her position and effectively blocking Alison's exit. "Don't lie to me."

Shoulders slumped, she looked away, regret bubbling hot and thick in her stomach. "I can't stay here."

"Why not?"

"I just can't." She exhaled slow and squeezed her eyes shut. *Damn.* She was so tired of running, of hiding, of lying to the people she cared about most.

But Copernatech wouldn't stop coming, wouldn't stop searching for her, wouldn't care if they took out hundreds of innocent lives to silence the whistleblower who'd escaped. Sometimes she almost wished she'd just kept her damned mouth shut about everything.

Almost.

Then again, the numbers said it was better to sacrifice one life to save thousands of others.

Too bad it was her life that had to be the one to go.

She sank down onto the sofa, as if the weight of all the months of living in secrecy were too much to bear. "I'm running from something."

"That's obvious." Faye took a seat beside her. "What is it? Abusive boyfriend?"

"I wish." Alison buried her face in her hands. "A boyfriend I could handle. No. This is much, much worse and if they find me, it won't just be me who's in danger. It'll be everyone I know too."

Faye snorted. "Sounds like a bad action-movie plot. Seriously, I'm sure he's not that bad. How do you know he's still even looking for you?"

Alison peered up at her friend from between her fingers. She apparently still thought it was a man after her. Another lie, but perhaps one that would keep her friend safe. Resigned, she straightened and dropped her hands into her lap, swallowing hard to push the knot of tension in her throat deeper inside. "I know because a mutual friend warned me."

Never mind this "mutual friend" had put her own life on the line by still working at Copernatech while feeding Alison information. That thought was followed closely by another—one that made her stomach sink to her toes. In her haste to get out of town, she'd forgotten to check under the bench for a new envelope. But since she was leaving anyway, it didn't really matter if Copernatech had figured out where she was.

She shifted in her seat and crossed her legs away from Faye. *Didn't matter.* Once she reached a new city, she'd have to send word to her contact to set up a new drop point anyway. That was always difficult. So far they'd been lucky. She'd either been close enough that Carolyn could make the drop, or Carolyn had had trusted family that she could mail the letter to who would put it in a place for Alison to grab. Once she moved on, she'd have to find a new go-between as well.

Faye continued to watch her with a narrowed gaze, her expression far too knowing for Alison's comfort. "Know what I think? I think you're leaving because you're scared. Period. Not because someone's after you, but because you're terrified."

"You don't know what you're talking about."

"Don't I? You don't open up to anyone. You never show any vulnerability. In fact, I think you're really leaving because of Owen."

Alison pushed to the far corner of the sofa and gave her friend a dubious look. "Don't be ridiculous. Whatever happened or didn't happen between us was a mistake. Nothing more."

"Right." Faye shook her head and grinned. "And I suppose that mistake is why your face is flushed and your eyes are sparkling. Nope. I think you're running now because you're afraid of getting too close."

She shrugged and stared out the window across the room. "I'm not afraid of that."

"Really?" Faye's tone turned curious. "Why's that? Did something happen already between the two of you?"

She didn't answer. No point in arguing anyway.

"I thought so." Faye clapped excitedly. "Oh, this could be good. This could be exactly what you need to heal from whatever you're running from. You can't let fear run your life."

"Fear's all I've got these days." Alison pushed to her feet, slinging her heavy duffle over her shoulder once more and heading for the door before Faye could stop her. "I need to get out of here."

"Fine. Go. If that's what you want." Faye trailed behind her, her voice carrying a hint of taunt. "Be a coward and leave your friends behind to suffer. But you at least should say goodbye to Owen and let him know you're leaving."

Despite her better judgment, Alison glanced back at her best friend over her shoulder, only to find Faye's cell phone front and center in her vision. On-screen was Owen's contact information.

Damn.

With her near-eidetic memory, those digits were now forever burned into her brain. Emotional blackmail, that's what it was. The worst kind of all. She shook her head and walked out into the hall as fast as her feet would take her. No looking back again. "Bye, Faye. Take care."

It was better this way, really. A clean break. No chance of the ones she left behind looking for her, calling in the authorities. Putting up missing person posters. That had happened once before and it had been a nightmare.

Nope.

Clean and quick was definitely the way to go.

She took the elevator down to the lobby and walked out into the bright Nevada day. Decision made, she hailed a cab and gave the driver the directions. She'd check the bench, just to know if they were on her trial. Knowledge was power, after all. But either way, this would be her last day in Vegas.

Across town, Owen picked up his cell phone for the millionth time, then tossed it down again and rubbed his eyes. He hadn't dated anyone in years, but vaguely remembered some rule about calling a woman too soon. Only problem with that theory was he'd never actually gotten said woman's phone number. Over a full day had passed since he'd last seen Alison. That had to be enough time, right? Then again, maybe it was too long. Maybe he'd royally screwed himself and lost any hope of a lasting relationship with her. But still, there was something about her that was off. He sensed there was something holding her back, something in her past and until he figured out what that was their relationship could never go anywhere.

"Mr. Rockford is in a meeting, sir," the receptionist at Rockford Security said. "Do you have an appointment?"

No. I don't have an appointment.

What he did have was an urgent need to get Blake to help him find out more about Alison's mysterious past. "I can wait, if he won't be long."

"Have a seat along the wall and I'll let him know you're here as soon as he's free." She gave him a polite smile and he headed to the oversized brown leather arm chairs.

He'd no more than plopped his butt down in one of them when an office door down the hall opened and Liv stepped out with Peaches. "Oh, hey cuz. Glad you're here. Saves me a trip to your apartment."

She released the dog's leash and Peaches immediately rushed to Owen's side, panting and happy and playful. Warmth burst in his chest and he realized he'd missed the pooch. Missed having another heartbeat around his lonely apartment and someone who was always happy to see him waiting by the door when he got home.

Perhaps it was the whole cheating debacle at the Lucky Ace. Perhaps it was the time he'd spent with Alison. Hell, perhaps he was just getting soft in his old age. Whatever it was, he'd made his decision—right then and there.

Peaches belongs with me. I'll adopt her this afternoon.

After he talked to Blake and discovered more about Alison, of course.

"Hey." Liv moved to stand on the other side of him. "What happened with that girl the other day?"

"Oh." Owen looked up at her between doggy kisses. "Alison, you mean? She's why I'm here. I was hoping your brother could help me get her phone number."

"Phone number, huh?" Liv's tone turned conspiratorial. "I can get it for you. It's a simple search and IT gave all the managers access. Just come in my office for a second."

"Great. Thanks." He took Peaches by the leash and led her back down the hall.

"I need the spelling of her first and last name and date of birth."

Owen closed his eyes bringing back the image of her license the day Peaches had stolen it in the casino. The license had her birth date. Owen rattled off the information and Liv typed it into the computer.

"Great. It'll take a minute or two to run through the system."

"Okay." He took a seat in one of the chairs in front of her desk and pulled out his cell phone again. "Sorry. I need to make a quick call."

After thumbing in the number, he leaned back, grateful to have a purpose other than Alison for the call.

"Paws and Play Animal Rescue. This is Shelby. How may I help you?"

"Hey, it's Owen." He gave his new pet a scratch behind the ears. "I want to adopt Peaches."

"Wow! Okay, great, but that's quite a change of heart. What made you decide?"

A weird constriction tightened his throat and chest with emotion. He coughed and lowered his voice, turning away from Liv who avidly watched him from across the desk. "You were right. I do need someone in my life."

"Aw. Well, I'm glad I could help. And you can have a human someone too, you know. You're a great catch."

He scoffed.

Yeah, right. The only woman I've been seriously interested in since Faith couldn't get out of my place fast enough.

"I'll dig up your paperwork from before and you can stop by the shelter later and sign it, okay?"

"Great. Thanks, Shelby."

Blake stuck his head through Liv's open doorway after Owen ended the call.

"Hey. I thought I heard your voice." Blake walked in, his trusty iguana perched on his shoulder, and handed him an envelope. "Here."

Peaches jumped up to sniff the reptile's twitching tail and Owen barely had time to catch her before she went after Henry like a real, live squeaky toy. He kept a firm grip on the dog's collar as he sat back in his chair. "What's this?"

"Another drop-off from that bus hut bench. One of

our guards at the casino, Steve, found it after they caught the cheaters."

Owen's chest tightened. He'd almost forgotten about the envelope. If Alison wasn't mixed up in something nefarious then why was she getting random envelopes from underneath public benches? What in the world was she in to?

"And no one opened it yet?" He ripped open the top and peered inside. "Why not?"

"Figured it was your case, you should do the honors." Blake gave Henry several air kisses then glanced down at Owen. "So?"

Owen pulled out a sheet of paper and scowled at the one sentence typed dead center. "It's sunny in Seattle." He wrinkled his nose. "What the hell does that mean?"

"Hmm." Blake frowned. "Some kind of code maybe?"

"Maybe." He held the paper up for Blake. "The rest is nothing but chit-chat. Mom is fine. Went to the grocery store. Ellen baked your favorite apple pie. And there's no postmark on the envelope or signature. Definitely not normal pen-pal stuff."

Blake took the paper from him and squinted at it. "I'll have my team analyze it to see if they can decipher anything."

"I've got more bad news," Liv said from behind her desk.

Owen's heart sank, all joy over his pending adoption of Peaches taking a backseat to the continued cloak-and-dagger stuff with Alison. "Let me guess, you can't find her phone number."

"Worse. The Alison James you gave me, with that birth date, died a week after birth. It's a fake identity. Whoever that girl was at your casino, her real name is not Alison James."

Flashes of the past—Faith and all her lies, his trial for suspected treason, all the guilt, the shame, the daily burden of knowing he'd trusted the wrong woman and been played for a sucker—slammed into him like a Mac truck.

But Alison wasn't Faith. The connection he'd felt with Alison was real. He'd spent only one night with her, but in that night something long dead inside him had come to life. She'd inspired his belief in her and himself again. He knew she had a secret, but it didn't make sense that she was just playing him like Faith had. For what? There was no reason for Alison to pretend to get close to him in order to garner information or some kind of advantage. Heck she'd even begged off on his dinner invitation *and* she'd helped them catch the cheater and even gotten injured in the process. No, something else was going on and if his gut instincts were correct, Alison was in grave danger.

"You okay?" Liv sat forward her expression concerned. "You don't look so good, cuz."

"I'm fine." He forced the words past his tight vocal cords and pushed to his feet. At least now he knew why

Alison had acted so strangely. An overwhelming urge to help her, to protect her came over him. But first he had to *find* her.

———

A FEW HOURS LATER, Owen paced the parking lot behind his apartment building near the Lucky Ace with Peaches' leash in one hand and holding his cell phone to his ear with the other. It might be the dog's potty break, but that didn't mean he couldn't multi-task.

"What do you mean she's gone?" He asked Faye, who was on the other end of the line, doing his best to keep his agitation from his tone. "Where is she?"

"I don't know. She stopped by here to get her laptop and didn't say where she was going. All I know is she had her duffle bag packed and my guess is she's probably looking for a way out of town."

"Why? Why would she leave like that?" He stopped near a sapling while Peaches did her business, squinting through his aviator shades into the bright afternoon sun. "What's she hiding, Faye?"

"I don't know, Mr. Rockford. I swear. All she told me was she was running from something."

"Running?" *Shit.*

He walked two paces then stopped again as Peaches found another spot to mark. "And stop with all the Mr.

Rockford crap. I think it's time you called me Owen, don't you? Considering the circumstances."

"Okay, Owen. Is Alison in trouble? I'm worried about her."

"So am I." He gave Peaches' leash an impatient tug to keep her from obsessively sniffing until midnight and started back toward his apartment. "That's why I need to find her. Whatever she's mixed up in, she needs my help."

Owen stopped near the entrance to the building and promised Faye he'd do what he could to find Alison then ended the call. He'd just shoved the phone back into his pocket and was reaching for the door handle when Peaches woofed loud and yanked hard on her leash, causing him to lose his grip. Before he could catch her, she'd taken off around the corner of the building.

"Dammit! Come back here." He raced after the dog only to damned near rundown a person on the other side of the wall. Owen stopped short and stared at the woman who'd been foremost in his thoughts for days. "Alison? What are you doing here? I've been looking all over for you."

She straightened from petting Peaches and tucked an errant curl behind her ear. She kept her gaze lowered, seemingly fascinated by the toes of her sneakers. "Can we, um, go somewhere and talk?"

"I know you're in trouble." He placed a hand on her

shoulder, as if to confirm she was really there and not a beautiful illusion. "Let me help."

Alison looked up at him then, and Owen's heart kicked into overdrive at the blatant fear in her expression.

What the hell is she mixed up in?

"Not here." She glanced around as if expecting a sniper to take her out any second. "Upstairs. Please?"

14

Outside Owen's door, Alison shuffled her feet and did her best to keep from fidgeting. All this was new—trusting someone, sharing her real past with someone, not constantly looking over her shoulder to be sure she wasn't followed.

While Owen fiddled with his keys, she scratched Peaches behind the ears. It had been months and her contact, Caroline, had nothing but the same report over and over. All clear.

Yesterday, there had been no envelope under the bench, a sign that it was still clear. Their arrangement was that a note would come every two weeks unless there was an emergency. The last regular envelope was just over a week ago, so she was still in the clear, but it had taken her almost twenty-four hours to wrestle with the decision of whether or not to trust Owen. Her head said no, but her heart said yes. In the end, her heart won out.

Maybe Copernatech had stopped looking for her, finally. Maybe once they'd driven her away from everything she'd known, they'd decided she was no longer a risk. Maybe they figured she was already dead.

"C'mon." Owen opened the door. "Let's get inside and talk."

Alison led the dog into his apartment then unclipped Peaches' leash and removed her hoodie, wanting to be as comfortable as possible for this completely uncomfortable conversation. She curled up on a corner of his sofa and toed off her shoes before tucking her feet beneath her. "I'm not sure where to start."

"I am." He discarded his suit jacket and loosened his tie before taking off his shoes and sitting opposite her, his brown gaze narrowed. "How about starting with who you really are."

"What?" Her pulse notched higher.

He knows about that? Of course he knows about that, idiot. He's in security.

Memories of him picking up her wallet that day at the casino, his slight hesitation as he stared at the holder where her license was kept on the back side, bombarded her brain.

"You heard me." He stretched his arm along the back of the cushions and watched her with an unreadable expression. "Alison James died a week after she was born."

"You memorized my information that day, didn't you?"

He didn't answer.

Brows knitted, she stared at her hands in her lap. She should've expected him to figure it out sooner or later. Better now, she supposed, if she intended to stay. "You ran a background check too."

It wasn't a question, since she already knew the answer.

Owen crossed his arms and tilted his head to the side, his tone flat. "I like to know who I'm getting involved with. You have a problem with that?"

"We're not involved." She glanced up at him then looked away fast. "Not yet, anyway. If you want me to leave, I will."

"What I want is the truth, goddammit." He raked a hand through his hair "What I want is to help you get rid of whatever you're running from."

"It's a long story."

"You have something better to do?"

No. I don't.

Truth was, it felt so good just to be with him again it scared the hell out of her. She shifted in her seat and drew her knees in closer. "I'll change the names to protect the innocent."

"I'd prefer you didn't."

"Knowing the truth could put you in danger."

"Honey, I thrive on danger. Four years in the Marines will do that to a guy. And I learned the hard way the importance of keeping secrets."

Well, then. She wanted to ask him more, but now wasn't the time. Not with the way he'd grown defensive after his last statement and her promise to tell him the truth and nothing but the truth.

After a deep breath, she started. "My real name is Heather Connors." She gave a small, sad smile. "God, it feels weird to say that now. Anyway, in my former life, I was a mathematician for a pharmaceutical company named Copernatech. My main focus was working as part of a team researching a new cancer vaccine. My duties specifically were to run the numbers associated with patient side effects, adverse effects, and deaths from the vaccine and determine probabilities of frequency as they moved forward through the clinical trials necessary for FDA approval." She picked nervously at the hem of her gray hoodie, the jolt of adrenaline caused by her discovery just as sickening now as it had been all those months ago. "Except their vaccine caused more deaths than it prevented, causing patients' immune systems to lower to dangerous levels or stop altogether—unacceptable results. When I took my data to the company execs, though, they brushed it aside and told me they'd handle it appropriately. They didn't. In fact, they accelerated the release date and sent falsified reports to the FDA to expedite the approval process."

Peaches jumped up on the sofa between them and settled down with her head on Alison's leg as if for moral support. She stroked the dog's soft head while she continued. "I couldn't let them harm or even kill all those people because of their greed. So I took the information to a reporter in the area who specialized in investigative journalism. It was all supposed to be anonymous. No one would get hurt, the drug would get pulled. End of story. But it wasn't the end. Not at all."

Peaches whimpered and Owen sat forward, his expression morphing from stoic to concerned. "I'm not liking where this is going."

"Believe me, I didn't either." She twisted a lock of hair around her finger. "Right before the story was set to run on the local network affiliate, the reporter turned up dead. The coroner ruled it a suicide, but I knew the truth. The guy had a great home, happy family, two kids in school. No way would he kill himself like that." She jammed her hands in the pocket of her hoodie so he wouldn't see them shake. "Then my house got broken into. They took my laptop, my devices, all the notes I'd kept on the vaccine project. Nothing else. And that's when I knew. I'd always known the pharmaceutical business was cut-throat. I'd just never imagined Copernatech would branch out into actual murder. I was wrong. So I ran. Found people to supply fake IDs and assumed the name of a deceased infant. That's when I became Alison James." She shrugged. "The only person I have any contact with from those days is a woman named Caroline Biggs who still works as a microbiologist at Copernatech. She keeps me informed if anyone from the company has discovered my location. Right now, I'm just trying to stay alive until I can come forward with what I know about that vaccine and stop it from ever reaching the light of day."

An awkward silence fell once she'd finished, only the sound of Peaches' tail thumping against the cushions filling the air and for once, Alison didn't have the guts to look at Owen for fear of what she'd see.

Disapproval? Most likely. Disappointment? Quite possibly.

Disgust?

She wouldn't blame him for being disgusted, she'd stolen the identity of an innocent baby to save herself, gone underground like a coward, retreated when she should've charged forward to prevent a catastrophe.

"Wow." Owen exhaled and rubbed a hand over his face. "What about the casino?"

"What about it?"

"Why were you at the Lucky Ace?"

"With all the risks, getting a job to support myself is impossible. So I put the skills I have to good use."

"You always intended to run the next time things got dicey?"

"Yeah. A girl's got to survive."

"What about Faye? She's your friend. That's a big risk with your past, right?"

Alison laughed. "Have you ever tried denying Faye what she wants?"

Owen chuckled. "Yeah, I have actually. Not exactly easy."

"No, it's not. Once that girl sets her mind on something, she gets it. She wanted me as her friend and she got me."

"Right." He took her hand, the one resting on Peaches' back, and held firm. "Anything else I need to know about you?"

"I think that's enough, don't you?"

He laced their fingers together and leaned back. Peaches jumped down and wandered over to her bowls in the kitchen. Owen pulled her closer to him and she went without resistance, cuddling up into his side. She'd never felt safer, more protected, more cared for..

Alison buried her nose in his chest and inhaled deeply of his spicy, clean scent. Owen wove the fingers of his free hand through her hair and grinned. "So, what should I call you? Alison? Heather?"

She straightened and did her best to get a hold of herself. "I like Alison. She feels like me now. I'm a different person than I was at Copernatech."

"Okay. Alison it is." He pulled her close again, seemingly missing her as much as she missed him. His deep voice rumbled through his chest beneath her ear. "I have one more question."

"All right?" The hint of hurt in his voice made her worries soar once more. Her own words emerged more hesitant than she'd wanted. "Go ahead."

"What happened between us... Was that a lie too?"

She sat up and placed her hand over his heart, the steady beat grounding her in the connection between them. "No. That was all truth."

Owen cupped her cheek and ran his thumb along the high ridge of her cheekbone. "You do care about me, at least a little, then?"

"A little?" She nuzzled into his palm and placed a kiss there before snorting. "More like a concave up function."

He scrunched his nose and gave her an impassive stare. "Sorry. I'm too mathematically challenged to know what the hell that means."

"It means they're constantly increasing." She giggled and dropped a kiss on his lips.

"So, yes?"

"Yes." If she was honest, she'd gone well past like days ago and was now on a direct collision course with love where Owen Rockford was concerned.

Not that she'd tell him. Not yet.

Not until she dealt with her past and knew where he stood on their future together.

This time when she kissed him, it was long and deep, expressing all the words and feelings she couldn't say.

Minutes later, when they both came up for air, Owen whispered, "Stay with me tonight. Tomorrow, we'll go to Blake's and get his help. He'll be able to get a clear handle on your situation. I'll keep you safe, I promise."

Her breath caught at the possibilities he offered—a future, a relationship, a real life again. She wanted those things, with him, more than anything in the world, but wouldn't allow herself to believe they were possible yet.

Tonight though? One night I can do.

"Okay." Alison rested her forehead against Owen's and looked deep into his warm brown gaze as her stomach rumbled. "I'd like that. But first, can you feed me?"

"GOD, THAT SMELLS AMAZING!" Alison peeked around Owen's side an hour later and snatched a slice of green pepper from the pile. "What is it again and when will it be ready?"

"Steak stir-fry and a few more minutes." He slapped her hand away as she went back to snatch another bite. "I can't believe you're still hungry after all the bites you've stolen."

"I'm starved." She pressed a kiss between his shoulder blades. "Did you know a statistician can have his head in an oven and his feet in ice, and he'll say on average he feels fine?"

"Is that another bad math joke?"

"It's a very good math joke, actually."

"Whatever you say."

"I say." She giggled.

He narrowed his eyes at her, one hand still on the handle of the pan. "I wonder…"

The way he looked at her made her nervous. "What? What do you wonder?"

"What you looked like as a kid."

"Ugh." She leaned forward and rested her head against his chest, right over his heart, enjoying the steady, reassuring thump, thump, thump of his pulse. Although it was a ploy to hide her flaming face, she relaxed the moment his free arm settled around her. "Believe me, nothing to write home about."

"Was your hair always this red?" He picked up a curl and twined it around his fingers.

"Yeah. I used to get made fun of for it all the time. Well, that and my brain."

"People made fun of your brain?" Owen raised his head to squint down at her. "I think your brain's amazing. I don't understand half of what comes out of your mouth, but it's still amazing."

She giggled and kissed his chest. "Thanks. It's okay. I'm over it now. It's just hard being the different kid, you know?"

"Yeah, I know." From the sad note in his voice, she got the sense that he did. She wanted to ask more, but his stomach grumbled loud this time and he laughed. "You ready for dinner?"

"Is a forty-five-degree angle acute?"

"Pretty sure I remember the answer from high school geometry." He tossed her a grin and pulled the pan off the stove. "But I'll take that as a yes."

15

───────

Alison awoke to the sound of scratching.

Squinting into the pre-dawn grayness, she spotted Peaches standing near the door. Beside her, spooned against her back, all warm and delicious, was Owen, His soft snores echoed as she propped up on one elbow and pushed the hair from her eyes. The warm weight of his arm around her felt like heaven on earth and she couldn't help saying a little prayer of thanks that she'd decided to talk to him, to finally open up and let someone in before taking off again.

Now, she had the possibility of a future, the possibility of love.

Now I have hope.

She cleared her throat and made kissy noises at the dog. "What's the matter, girl? Do you need to go outside, huh?"

Peaches padded over and whined.

"Okay." Alison stood and pulled on her clothes from the day before then quietly led the dog from the room so as not to wake Owen. "Let's find your leash and I'll take you downstairs."

After getting the dog ready, she slipped her feet into her sneakers and pulled on her hoodie before heading out of the apartment. She could only imagine her hair looked like some kind of crimson nightmare after sleeping and she hadn't taken the time to do more than run her fingers through it before leaving his place, but at this early hour, who cared?

The elevator took her and Peaches down to the lobby and she walked outside into the crisp air then around the corner to a small patch of grass with a tree near the curb. Owen's place was close enough to Fremont Street and the Lucky Ace that tourists still milled about and the traffic was as thick as it was at noon. This little side street, however, was blissfully deserted.

"C'mon, girl." She coaxed Peaches to get her business done faster while bouncing from foot to foot. "I don't know about you, but I'm chilly out here."

The dog obediently sniffed the tree trunk several times then chose her spot and squatted. Moments later, she kicked her back legs a few times then trotted excitedly, panting.

"What is it, girl?" Alison grinned down at Peaches then scratched her behind the ears. "Did you get your business done? Did you? That's such a good girl. Yes, it is."

A slight whistle sounded near her ear, followed by a spray of wood chips.

Wood chips? That's weird.

Confused, Alison straightened and looked around.

Another whistle sounded, followed by something hot grazing her shoulder.

What the...?

Several thoughts popped into her head simultaneously. First, there were now round holes in the tree trunk where before there'd been none. Second, her T-shirt stuck to her shoulder and something wet trickled down her skin like she'd been injured. Like she'd been shot.

Sharp stinging soon followed.

Oh. God.

I've been shot. Someone's shooting at me.

Copernatech!

She dove out of the way as a third bullet whizzed by and Peaches' leash slipped from her hand. The dog, ears back and tail down, bolted fast around the corner, leaving Alison alone.

Crap.

Pressed tight against the wall of the apartment building, she battled against her rising panic. They'd finally found her and of course they wanted her dead. She needed to run. She needed to hide. She needed to warn Owen and Faye so they'd be safe.

Think. Think. Think.

She leaned forward slightly and peered down the street. A hooded figure approached from around the corner, the streetlights glinting off the barrel of a gun, and for a moment she froze with fear.

Run. Hide. Escape.

Fight-or-flight took over in the nick of time and she raced away, her mind whirring with self-recriminations at near light-speed. She should've never been stupid enough to believe it was all over, that she was safe, that she might have the future of her dreams. Happy endings only happened in movies.

Throat tight and chest burning, she charged forward, tears in her eyes as she headed for the main street where there would be other people, hoping the assassin wouldn't shoot where anyone else was around. Forget the money she had stashed in her duffle. Forget Faye had been her best and closest friend in years. Forget the life she'd built here, the relationships, the love.

Worst of all, I never got to say goodbye.

Alison ran and ran and ran, without looking back. Block after block until she finally stopped and hazarded a look behind her. The bad guy was gone, for now giving her time to dwell on her next issue.

I've got nothing. No money. No ID. No phone.

She walked on for several more blocks, searching for a place to hide and think. At last, she came across an abandoned warehouse, its rusty door hanging from the hinges. She slipped inside and found a somewhat dry and clean place to crouch in the shadows. Every sound echoed off the corrugated steel walls, reminding her the danger was far from over. If she'd discovered this place, chances were good that others had too.

Others whose motives might not prove as honorable as hers.

The last thing she needed was to get mugged, especially since she didn't have anything. She pulled her hoodie tighter around herself and leaned back against the cool metal wall, the superficial wounds on her shoulder still seeping and aching. Without means, she wouldn't get far and honestly, she really didn't want to leave Vegas.

Before, it had always just been her, alone against the world.

Now, she had Faye and Owen and her apartment and Peaches and...

No. This time, I stay.

This time I'll make a stand against Copernatech and all the big corporate bullies of the world, exposing them for what they are: greedy cowards.

Pulling her knees into her chest, Alison rested her chin atop them and focused on what she still had. Her mind. Math was what she did best, so math is what she'd use to get her out of this mess.

The police would require proof that the pharmaceutical giant was behind the attack. They'd need to capture the thug who'd shot at her and any accomplices he might have. In order to make that happen, however, probability said she'd need something to draw them out.

I'll use myself as bait.

They were currently watching Owen's apartment building, so she needed to get them away from there to keep everyone safe, lure them to someplace where she'd have the upper hand, somewhere she'd have the advantage.

The Boneyard.

Her fear dissipated, replaced now by resolve. The boneyard was the place where old Vegas signs were retired. Giant hulks of rusted metal and broken neon crowded the lot. She'd scoped the place out shortly after arriving in Vegas, thinking it would be a perfect spot for an ambush, if the need ever arose.

Alison pushed to her feet and dusted off her hands on the thighs of her jeans.

Goal and plan in place, she headed for the warehouse door.

Yep. The time's here.

Time for Alison James to take her hard-earned life back.

---

*W*OOF. *Woof. Woof.*

Owen rolled over and slung his arm across his eyes.

The first streaks of sun were piercing through the bedroom curtains. He smiled despite the early hour and fumbled his hand over to the mattress beside him.

Empty.

Frowning, he lifted his arm and peered sideways at the vacant spot where Alison should've been. What the hell? He didn't even remember her getting up.

Scratch. Scratch. Scratch.

Groaning, he rolled out of bed and tugged on his jeans before padding to the bedroom door. He yanked it open, expecting Peaches to charge in, but nothing.

Weird. Owen walked down the hall, scowling as he approached the front door and the desperate canine whines grew louder. The apartment didn't have a doggy door, so how in the hell had Peaches gotten out?

He opened the door and the dog scrambled inside, slipping and sliding on the hardwood floor, trembling all over. Her leash trailed behind her in ominous warning. Alison must've taken her for a walk, but when he peered out into the hallway, there was no sign of Alison.

Peaches practically pawed a hole through his leg, so Owen crouched and did his best to calm her. "What's wrong, girl? Huh? Where's Alison?"

At the mention of her name, Peaches cried and Owen's heart tripped.

The stories she'd told him about her corrupt former employer and their shady tactics to the news of their failure silently resurfaced, cooling his blood to ice in his veins.

Have they finally found her? Have they taken her? Hurt her? Worse?

She'd said her contact had indicated it was all-clear. Had something changed? He'd never asked her just exactly how she communicated with her contact ... the envelope under the bench!

Things had heated up so fast between them the night before he'd never mentioned the envelope to Alison, but that must have been their method of communication. Alison thought it was all clear except she'd never gotten that last message because Blake's people had intercepted it. Had that message contained the code phrase that would have alerted Alison that Copernatech was onto her? Now she was in danger and it was *his* fault!

Straightening, he stalked into the kitchen and grabbed his cell phone from the charger. If anyone so much as damaged one hair on Alison's head, he'd murder them. Quickly, he thumbed the speed dial button for Blake and left a curt message then did the same on Liv's number. If someone had abducted Alison, the Rockfords were his best shot for getting her back.

While he waited for them to arrive, he took a quick shower and put on fresh jeans and a T-shirt then fixed a still nervous Peaches some breakfast before getting himself a much-needed cup of joe. Twenty minutes later, he answered a pounding on his door to find his cousins on the other side.

"I'll need to know everything, from the beginning." Blake charged in and took a seat on the sofa, letting Henry jump from his shoulder to the back cushions. "The whole truth."

"All I know is what she told me last night." Owen scrubbed a hand through his still damp hair and took a seat in an armchair across from Blake. "But I believe her."

"Good." Blake pulled out a tablet computer from inside his jacket. "Start with the basics."

"Her real name is Heather Connors. She's twenty-eight and holds a Master's Degree in mathematics. She worked for a pharmaceutical company named Copernatech, on a team working with a new cancer vaccine. She'd been hired to analyze the data from the clinical trials and determine results of success or failure as part of their FDA approval process. But she said they didn't like her interpretation of the data—the vaccine did more harm than good—and when she went to the execs about the potentially deadly side effects, they brushed her aside. At that point, she turned whistleblower and went to a reporter with the information. The reporter later turned up dead, before the story could break. Then she said the company broke into her home and stole all of her research and notes on the project. That's when

Alison went underground and she's been on the run ever since."

"All right." Blake frowned at his tablet screen, his thumbs flying across the screen as he typed in Owen's information. "I'm sending this to the IT team. If this checks out, we'll get to the bottom of everything. I promise."

"Thanks, man." He rubbed his eyes and bumped his shoulder against Liv, who'd taken a seat on the arm of his chair. "I really appreciate you both coming over here."

"No problem." Liv ruffled his hair. "That's what family's for."

"Right." He took his empty mug to the kitchen then paced the small living room. "Shit. I just feel like I need to do something, be out there looking for her, you know?"

"You're doing the best thing you can," Liv said. "Blake will handle it. Don't worry."

"Easy for you to say." He walked past the side table near the front door and noticed Alison's phone still lying there. He picked it up and stared at the screen, now covered with missed call alerts from Faye. "Damn."

He hit redial.

Faye answered on the second ring. "Where the hell are you, Al? I've been trying to reach you all night. People came to the casino asking about you and now I'm at your apartment and your bag's still here, so you haven't left town and—"

"Faye? It's Owen."

"Owen?" Her shock was evident in her tone. "Why do you have Alison's phone? What's going on?"

"Alison's disappeared. She left her phone at my place when she took off."

"But she doesn't go anywhere without her phone."

"I know." He took a deep breath and leaned back against the wall. "Listen, there are things about her you probably don't know."

"I know she's my best friend and I'm worried." A hint of anger joined the concern in her voice. "What more do I need to know?"

"That she's a whistleblower, against some very powerful, very dangerous people. And she's running for her life."

Silence followed—long enough that Owen checked the phone to make sure they were still connected. "Faye? Are you still there?"

"I'm here." Her words emerged quieter this time. "Jesus. I knew she was a math geek who can't hold her liquor and that she snorts when she laughs, but I never suspected anything like this. I thought she was hiding from an abusive boyfriend or something."

"The 'or something' part is right."

"What are we going to do, Owen? We have to help her. She's loyal to the bone and she's stuck her neck out for me more times than I can count. I won't let her face this alone."

"Neither will I." He pushed away from the wall, a new idea forming. "You said you're at her apartment?"

"Yeah."

"Great. Give me the directions and stay put. I'm coming over."

He jotted down the address then ended the call. Looking up, he found two nosy cousins staring back at him. "I've got to go out. Liv can you watch Peaches until I get back?"

"Sure."

"Need backup?" Blake watched him with a narrowed gaze.

"Nah, I got it." Owen shoved his feet into a pair of shoes and grabbed his keys off the side table. "Just wish me luck."

Fifteen minutes later, he swerved his sedan up to the curb in front of a sedate looking beige ranch house in a quiet suburban neighborhood. Not exactly where he'd expect to find a math genius with a dark past, but then again, that was probably Alison's plan.

That's my smart girl.

As he climbed out of the car and walked toward the basement entrance where Faye waited, he couldn't help but smile. Yep. Alison was his girl now. Maybe more, if she'd accept him into her life like he wanted to accept her into his.

And if they all survived this shitfest of a situation.

"Hey." He waited while Faye unlocked the apartment

door then walked inside. "You said people were asking for her at the Lucky Ace?"

"Yeah." Faye turned to close the door behind them only to stop as a little old lady stood on the stoop with a foil-wrapped dish in her hands. "Can I help you, ma'am?"

"I'm Ms. Baker, Alison's landlord." The woman looked between Owen and Faye, her expression wary. "Who are you two?"

"My name's Owen Rockford, ma'am." He plastered on his most polite smile and stepped forward to take the dish from the woman's hands. "And this is Alison's friend, Faye. We stopped by to speak with her, but she doesn't seem to be home. Any ideas where she might be?"

"No. She keeps to herself most of the time." Ms. Baker shook her head disapprovingly. "Such a sweet, pretty girl. I've told her over and over she needs to socialize more, find herself a good husband and settle down." She eyed Owen up and down. "Are you single, Mr. Rockford?"

"I'm seeing someone. Alison, in fact." He ignored the blatantly curious look on Faye's face and ushered the older woman back out the door. "Thanks so much for stopping by."

"Tell Alison to heat the chicken and dumplings I brought at three hundred seventy-five degrees for forty-five minutes and they'll perk right up."

"Will do." Owen gave the landlady an appreciative smile. "So nice to meet you, ma'am."

"And you, Mr. Rockford. That Alison's a lucky girl to find a nice boy like you."

"Thank you, ma'am. But I'm the lucky one."

He waited until Ms. Baker disappeared back into her apartment upstairs then closed the door and shoved the dish of leftovers in the fridge before turning to Faye once more. "Okay, back to the people at the casino. Can you describe them?"

"There were two. A tough looking guy then later it was a dark-haired woman."

"Notice anything remarkable or unusual about them?"

"You mean other than the fact they were looking for my best friend who's the most private, isolated person in the world? No."

"Great." His tone suggested the exact opposite. "All right. Well, help me look around the place. Maybe we can find a clue about where she is or where she was planning to go after she left Vegas."

A thorough search of the apartment, however, turned up nothing.

Frustrated, Owen headed back out into the living room. His phone buzzed and he pulled it out of his jeans pocket to see Blake's face onscreen. Answering, he paced to burn off some excess energy. "Please tell me you found something."

"Her story checks out. Heather Connors worked for Copernatech until just under a year ago. Alison's picture from the casino footage matches the ID they had on file for her."

"Okay, good. What else?"

Blake efficient tone turned less chipper. "One of my techs dug a little further into the situation and found one of the top executives from Copernatech landed at McCarran Airport three days ago."

"They're in Vegas? Shit." His heart nosedived to somewhere near his toes. Alison was most definitely in danger. "Can you track the bastard?"

"Already got people on it."

Owen ended the call and joined Faye in the kitchen. "That was Blake. He did some checking on Alison's background. Her story about the pharmaceutical company checks out."

"Like you didn't think it would?" Faye crossed her arms and gave him a full-on resting bitchface look. "Some boyfriend you are."

Before he could answer, his phone buzzed again, this time with a text.

THE NEON MUSEUM BONEYARD. MIDNIGHT. BRING POLICE.

IF I MISCALCULATED... JUST KNOW, I WANTED TO STAY.

A

"Shit." He squinted at the phone until the screen

went black. The message could have come from Alison, or it could be a trick. Either way it was the only lead they had on her whereabouts.

"What?" Faye stepped in beside him and tapped the screen to look at the message. "Oh, my God. You have to help her."

"What if it's not from Alison."

"What if it is?"

Owen took the phone back and pinged the message, his doubts only growing stronger when he discovered the message had originated from a less than savory part of town. The location was pretty far from his apartment and he couldn't imagine Alison going someplace so dangerous alone, unless taken there against her will—or desperate. He quickly called Blake and relayed the information about the text and location. It was probably sent from a burner phone, but Blake could trace it since Owen's phone messages went through Rockford Security servers.

Dammit. Faye was right. He couldn't not show up. It might be his only chance to save the woman who'd suddenly become the most important person in his life. He shoved the device back in his pocket and headed for the door. "I need to go."

"Wait." Faye dogged his footsteps. "I'm coming with you."

"Don't you have to work?"

"Don't you have more important things to worry

about than my schedule?"

Can't argue with that one.

"Fine. Whatever." Owen walked to his car while Faye locked up the apartment then joined him. "I can't guarantee your safety though."

"I can take care of myself, mister." She slid into the passenger seat and buckled her seat belt. "Don't worry about me. Where are we headed?"

He rattled off the address of the warehouse where Alison's text had originated from. Odds were slim she'd still be there, but he had to check. "Sounds like they arrived three days ago with the sole intent of finding Alison."

"Uh-oh."

Less than five minutes later, they squealed to a stop outside an abandoned dump of a building. Owen and Faye climbed out and joined Blake, who was already there. He turned to them as they approached. "Sorry. I've got a team still searching the area, but there's no sign of the exec or Alison. We did find a homeless guy passed out inside, but he couldn't tell us anything. Let me see her message."

Cursing, Owen pulled out his phone and showed Blake the text. Come hell or high water, he'd be at the Boneyard tonight. "I'm going."

"Could be a trap."

"Don't care. One way or another, I'm getting Alison back. Tonight."

16

———

Eleven forty-five.

Alison took a deep breath and stared at the clock on the wall at the twenty-four-hour coffee house in which she'd taken refuge. The crowds made her feel safer and the owners hadn't kicked her out, even though she'd been nursing the same cup of coffee for hours. She'd managed to scrounge enough money together by pawning her watch to buy the cheap burner phone she'd used to text Owen earlier, snag a fresh top and hoodie at a second-hand store to replace her bloodstained one and buy some bandaids. She'd tended to the injury in the ladies room (just a deep graze, thankfully) before scoring a muffin and mug of joe here to keep her going.

With luck, soon, I'll be free.

She sipped the last of her coffee before pushing to her feet and heading out into the open streets of Vegas again. Her best bet for picking up the Copernatech thug again was to return to Owen's apartment building, so she headed the few blocks over. If her plan had any hopes for success, she needed the gunman to follow her.

Fortunately, it didn't take long. After a mere ten minutes of pacing, the man approached her from around the corner again, his build and silhouette the same as the earlier shooter.

Bingo!

Pulse racing, she took off at a fast walk toward the Boneyard just north of Owen's place. The first time he'd shot at her, he'd waited until they were in a deserted side street, so this time she stuck to heavily populated areas and somehow refrained from breaking into a run. She didn't want to call attention to her or the gunman, if she did he might start shooting and an innocent person could get hurt.

Every so often, she'd glance over her shoulder to make sure he was still in pursuit.

Yep. Still there, lingering back maybe fifty-feet or so.

As she neared the entrance to the Neon Museum, she took an unexpected turn to the right and slipped into a shadowed alcove, hoping to lose him briefly to allow her to sneak past the museum's security and into the Bone-yard. Moments later, the guy stopped a few feet from her hiding place, his breath loud in the cool night air. Alison didn't move a muscle, eyes squeezed shut as she waited for him to either kill her or move away.

Thankfully, he cursed and walked back toward the main street.

Alison sagged against the brick wall then hesitated a bit longer before jogging the short distance to the Boneyard's employee side exit. The chain link gate was secured with only a heavy padlock. After what she had planned tonight, they'd change that soon enough, but for now it was perfect. She pulled out a bobby pin from her pocket and crouched to pick the lock.

Good thing self-defense wasn't the only thing she'd learned back in the dojo.

Minutes later, the tumblers inside the padlock slipped into place and the top popped open. Alison straightened and shoved the pin back into her pocket, only to feel a hand on her shoulder.

Fuck.

She'd done her best to keep a lookout while picking the lock, but she must've gotten distracted. Breath held, she turned slowly to face whoever was behind her, well aware these might be her last moments on earth.

Except the face that came into view wasn't the thug who'd followed her, but a familiar one, a trusted one. She gave a relieved sigh. "Caroline, you scared the living crap out of me. What are you doing here?"

Her contact at Copernatech, Caroline Biggs, had served on the same team as Alison. She held a finger to her lips and glanced around, her short dark curls bouncing around her face. "Let's get inside first, where it's safe."

"Right." Alison creaked open the gate as quietly as possible and waved her friend through then followed behind. They walked to a large metal sign shaped like a cowboy boot and Alison leaned against it for a moment, head lowered. "We don't have a lot of time. There's a Copernatech thug on the loose."

"I know." Caroline's voice sounded odd. Alison looked up in time to see her draw a gun from inside her jacket. "How do you think I knew where to find you?"

Realization dawned with sickening clarity.

Caroline had turned on her for Copernatech.

Hands held up in the universal sign of surrender, Alison pushed away from the sign. If she played along, hopefully it might buy her some time to escape. "What's going on Caro? I thought we were in this together."

"We were, until Copernatech gave me no choice." Her bright smile faltered and tears gathered in her dark eyes. "I'm sorry about this, Heather. I tried to warn you in the letter five days ago, why didn't you run?"

"The last letter?" Alison thought back to the last time she'd been to the bench. There had been no letter. Had someone else gotten it first? "The last one I got was over a week ago."

A spark of contrition flashed through Caro's eyes, but the gun didn't waver. "I'm sorry. Really, I am. But they've got my family. My babies. If I don't hand you over, they'll kill them."

"I can help you, Caro." Alison inched slightly to the side. The place was a maze of old, abandoned signage. If she could get lost inside the bones of Old Las Vegas, the probability of her survival greatly increased. "I'm a mathematician, remember? Between the two of us, we can outsmart these guys. Just let me calculate some numbers."

"No." Caroline moved closer, the gun trembling in her hands. "No more calculations. No more outsmarting them. They won, Heather. It's over."

Given the distance between herself and Caro and the level of darkness, she should be able to fight her way out of this without doing any serious damage to either of them, at least in theory. Decided, Alison inhaled and gave a slight nod. "I'm sorry too, Caroline."

Before the other woman could react, Alison kicked the gun from her hands, followed by a fast blow to Caroline's chest and the side of her head. Caroline slumped unconscious at her feet. *Thank God for all those self-defense lessons.*

Adrenaline pumping and time short, she dragged the woman's body behind the gigantic steel boot then took off into the heart of the Boneyard. If they hadn't moved anything around since the last time she'd been here, there should be a spot near the middle of the maze that would give her optimal visual advantage over her opponent. Now, all she has to do is wait for him.

It didn't take long.

She crouched behind a large rectangular sign and held her breath as the sound of the metal gate squeaking open was followed by the crunch of footsteps on gravel.

Closer, closer...

The footfalls ceased and a gruff curse rang out through the pitch black night.

He must've found Caro.

The steps started again, louder and quicker this time, headed in her general direction.

Alison closed her eyes and concentrated on the impending approach of her attacker, ran through the logistics of it all in her head one more time.

Any minute now, any minute now, any minute...

Now!

She darted from cover and deeper into the maze of signs, leading the thug closer to where she needed him. This had to work or she'd be dead before Owen ever arrived.

Owen.

A pang of yearning stabbed her heart.

Where is he?

It had to be close to midnight now, given the angle of the moon above. Only a few more minutes and this would all be over. Only a few more minutes and...

The Copernatech thug stepped into the required

spot and Alison acted on pure instinct. With her left shoulder, she shoved hard against the nearest sign— once, twice—until it gave a low groan and teetered over, knocking into the next sign, which toppled into the next sign, and the next until she'd started a domino effect.

Soon, the entire Boneyard was filled with the *clang-clang* of colliding signage until all that remained was a heaping pile of debris and dust at the center of the space, trapping her attacker inside the mess.

She coughed and squinted over at the employee gate.

Still no Owen.

Had he decided not to come? Decided I'm not worth the risk?

As if on cue the wail of sirens neared and Alison grinned.

OWEN SLAMMED on his brakes just outside the gate to the Boneyard and jammed his car's transmission into Park. That damned traffic snarl on the Strip had made him later than he'd wanted. And maybe he was taking up three parking spaces. Right now, he didn't care if he was blocking the whole fucking lot for the police that followed. The woman he loved was inside that fence— possibly hurt and definitely in danger—and he sure as hell planned to get her out.

As a steady stream of squad cars filled the roadway

behind him, Owen stalked over to the gate and kicked it open, Rambo-style.

The first thing he saw when he entered was a large cloud of dust erupting from the center of the Boneyard. The second was a pale arm stretched out on the ground from behind a rusted cowboy boot sign.

Heart in his throat, he charged over to the body, praying hard it wasn't Alison. Cautiously, he peered around the edge of the sign and spotted a mop of dark brown hair. Relieved, he knelt beside the unconscious woman.

Not dead either.

Good.

He checked her pulse once more to be sure, then stood and pulled a Glock 9mm from the holster at his hip. He had a license to carry, but rarely used it these days unless necessary.

Tonight was most definitely necessary.

Sticking close to a row of still-upright signage for cover, he inched down one of the rows and headed for the creaking pile of crap at the center of the field. From the looks of most of this shit around here, all of it could come crashing down at any second. All the noise and dust and high-octane buzz of adrenaline took him straight back to his combat days, but he shoved those memories aside. Now wasn't the time to get lost in the past.

Now was the time to find Alison and make sure she was safe.

The metallic tang of rust stung his nose as he crept closer to what he could now see was a huge pile of fallen signs. Jesus, somebody sure as hell did a number on those things. They were piled up at least twenty feet high and those ominous groans and moans weren't helping either.

Flashes of red and blue lights from the cop cars broke through the shadows and soon the ominous groans and moans from the pile were joined by the sounds of police moving into place and radio communications.

Owen exhaled and continued forward. Somewhere in this maze of chaos was the bastard who'd abducted Alison. He wanted to call out for her, to make sure she was okay, but he didn't want to give away his position either. Finally, he reached the center of the Boneyard and stopped for a moment to just take it all in.

It was quieter here. In fact, if he leaned in and listened hard he could almost hear…

Scowling, Owen took a step back.

That sounds like a curse.

He leaned in again and grinned.

Yep. Definitely a string of obscenities that would make most sailors blush.

Based on the gruff tone, a man was trapped in there and whoever the hell he was he was *not* happy about it.

Owen clicked on the safety on his gun and stashed it in its holster then stepped forward to lift up the edge of one of the signs to check beneath it.

"Don't do that!"

Whipping around, he spotted Alison a few feet away. Tangled hair hung in her eyes, dirt and rust smudged her clothes and face, and still she was the most beautiful sight he'd ever seen.

She stepped around a large letter N and shook her head. "He'll get out and I don't want him to get out until the cops are here. According to my calculations, he's fine anyway. Just trapped."

Owen straightened and moved closer. "According to your calculations, huh?"

"Yes." Alison blew a stray strand of hair away from her eyes. "If you take the maximum energy and divide it by the force needed to create the level of momentum necessary for…"

Unable to resist any longer, Owen rushed forward and pulled her into a tight embrace, bringing his lips down on hers to silence any further math mumbo-jumbo.

Alison's here. Alison's alive. Alison's in my arms where she belongs.

Eventually, he cupped her face in his hands, looking her over for any signs of injury. "Are you okay? Did he hurt you at all?"

"I'm fine." She pulled free, her tone slightly

perturbed. "Despite the hiccup in my plan. I made it work though."

Owen pulled her in for another passionate kiss, leaving them both breathless. "I thought I was going to lose you."

"I'm sorry. After he shot at me and Peaches got away, it was too risky to contact you until I had a plan in mind. Unfortunately, it turns out they were blackmailing my contact, Caroline. They took her family hostage and told her they'd kill them all if she didn't lead them to me."

"Caroline?"

"The woman out front. I feel bad about knocking her out, but what else could I do. She's okay, isn't she?"

"Yes." Owen chuckled. Only Alison would be sorry about knocking out someone who was trying to kill her. "I checked on her on my way over here. She was still out, but her pulse was strong and her breathing regular." He swore under his breath and gave her a little shake. "You scared the bejesus out of me though. I thought that was you lying there."

"Oh." She frowned. "I didn't take that probability into consideration. Sorry. It wasn't my intention to scare you. In fact, about the second part of that text. I—"

Whatever she'd been about to say was cut off by his kiss. The reminder of the danger she'd been in made him desperate to keep her close. This time when he pulled away, his throat felt tight with emotion. "I'm just glad you're okay."

She swiped a lock of hair away from his forehead then relaxed against him, tucking her head under his chin. For several moments, they just held each other, rocking back and forth slowly until his thudding heart eventually slowed to a normal rhythm. Alison leaned back, her expression concerned. "What about Peaches? Did she find her way home?"

"Yep. Came right back to me."

"Smart girl." Alison raised herself up on tiptoes and kissed him lightly.

The sound of a clearing throat stopped him from deepening the kiss. He stepped back from Alison, but kept her hand in his as he turned to find Blake standing nearby along with several police officers.

"Sorry to interrupt, but these gentlemen need to get your statement, Ms. James." Blake hiked a thumb at one of the men beside him. "If you have a moment."

"Of course." She pointed at the stack of rubble behind her. "They might want to get the bad guy out from under there first though."

"Right." One of the officers radioed in and soon a crew of cops arrived to lift the signs off the trapped assailant. "We'll take it from here, Mr. Rockford."

"Good." Blake gestured for Owen and Alison to follow him away from the scene. "The ambulance is here for you as well, Alison, in case you have any injuries."

"I'm fine, really." A pair of EMTs rushed over anyway

to cover Alison with a blanket and take her vitals. "Honest. Just a scratch on my shoulder from earlier."

Owen stayed by her side the whole time, unwilling to let her out of his sight for a second until they had that creep beneath the signs securely in police custody. Finally, the EMTs cleared her and they joined Blake near the employee side gate to the Boneyard.

"Your friend, Ms. Biggs, regained consciousness and I was able to ask her a few questions," Blake said as they approached.

"Did you?" Alison said, grasping Owen's hand a bit tighter.

"Yep. I convinced her it would be in her best interest to turn on Copernatech. Based on the nature of this case and the fact it crosses state lines, local law enforcement should be able to get her assigned to the U.S. Marshall's office and Witness Protection will guard her and her family from this point forward."

"I see."

Her quiet tone had Owen tugging her closer into his side. "That's good. That means she can stop running and so can you."

"It also means you can return to being Heather Connors," Blake said, glancing at Alison. "If that's what you want."

She dug the toe of her sneaker into the gravel. Owen slipped his arm around her waist and gave her a reassuring squeeze. "Whatever you want. I'll be here to support you either way."

Finally, she shook her head. "I've changed too much this past year. Whoever Heather Connors was, that isn't me anymore. Alison James is who I am now."

"Okay." Blake nodded. "Alison James it is then. You know, Alison, I could use a talented mathematician on my team at Rockford Security."

"Yeah? Doing what? Security isn't exactly my specialty."

"You'd be surprised at the different assignments that come our way. Anyway, keep it in mind if you're planning on sticking around Las Vegas for a while." Blake frowned and pulled his buzzing cell phone from his pocket. "Sorry. Excuse me, but I have to take this."

Owen watched his cousin walk away, his gut knotted with tension. He wanted Alison to stay more than he wanted his next breath, but he wouldn't force her. It had to be her decision, her choice.

She glanced up at him and grinned. "Why so glum?"

"Nothing."

"I am you know."

"What?"

"Sticking around." She faced him and took both of his hands in hers. "Meeting you was like a switch to polar coordinates: complex and imaginary things were given a magnitude and a direction."

"That's another weird math analogy I'll never get, isn't it?"

Alison laughed and raised up on her tiptoes, her warm breath tickling his face as her lips hovered millimeters from his. "Maybe you'll understand this."

As her lips captured his in a fiery kiss, Owen moaned deep in his throat and pulled her tight against him, loving the feel and taste and smell of her.

Loving Alison. Period.

Yep. *That* he understood perfectly.

THE END.

HAVE you read the Sam Mason Mysteries yet?

Start with book 1 *Telling Lies* - Small town cops and their K-9, Lucy, fight for justice in a town full of secrets and lies:

TELLING LIES

JOIN my readers list to get new release notifications:
http://ladobbs.com/newsletter

DID you know that I write mysteries under other names?
Join the LDobbs reader group on Facebook and find out!
It's a fun group where I give out inside scoops on my
books and we talk about reading!
https://www.facebook.com/groups/ldobbsreaders

ALSO BY L. A. DOBBS

Sam Mason Mysteries

***

Telling Lies (Book 1)

Keeping Secrets (Book 2)

Exposing Truths (Book 3)

Betraying Trust (Book 4)

Killing Dreams (Book 5)

More books in the Rockford Security Series:

Cold As Her Heart

A Game of Kill

No One To Trust

No Time To Run

Don't Fear The Truth

Hide From The Past

ABOUT THE AUTHOR

L. A. Dobbs also writes light mysteries as USA Today Bestselling author Leighann Dobbs. Lee has had a passion for reading since she was old enough to hold a book, but she didn't put pen to paper until much later in life. After a twenty-year career as a software engineer, she realized you can't make a living reading books, so she tried her hand at writing them and discovered she had a passion for that, too! She lives in New Hampshire with her husband, Bruce, their trusty Chihuahua mix, Mojo, and beautiful rescue cat, Kitty.

Her book "Dead Wrong" won the "Best Mystery Romance" award at the 2014 Indie Romance Convention.

Her book "Ghostly Paws" was the 2015 Chanticleer Mystery & Mayhem First Place category winner in the Animal Mystery category.

Join her VIP Readers group on Facebook:
https://www.facebook.com/groups/ldobbsreaders

Find out about her L. A. Dobbs Mysteries at:
http://www.ladobbs.com

This is a work of fiction.

None of it is real. All names, places, and events are products of the author's imagination. Any resemblance to real names, places, or events are purely coincidental, and should not be construed as being real.

CALCULATING DESIRES

Copyright © 2016-2020

L. A. Dobbs

All Rights Reserved.

No part of this work may be used or reproduced in any manner, except as allowable under "fair use," without the express written permission of the author.

❀ Created with Vellum